MUSCLE

DAVID BARRY

THAMES RIVER PRESS

For Carol, and with fond memories of Martyn

1

BONEBREAKING

I'm not addicted to coke and sometimes go weeks without a hit. But occasionally, when it feels like it's going to be a long night, I like to liven up the old grey cells a bit.

I leant over the porcelain top of the cistern and sniffed the line through a twenty. First an acid sting in the eyes followed by a sudden awakening as I raised my head and stared at my reflection in the mirror of the bathroom cabinet. I don't know what I expected to see but the face that stared back at me had worn reasonably well. Not bad, in spite of my lifestyle. I'm reasonably pleased with the way I look, which is not to say that I have a huge ego, but I'm satisfied with my good head of hair, even though the brown has turned to grey and the face might be just a little bloated. It's a face I like to think of as one with loads of expression and humour. Not bad for fifty-five. And the hit had given my lustreless grey eyes a blue sparkle, like precious stones twinkling in the mirror. But it would be a long night and the sparkle would plummet long before dawn. I might do a bit more around 3:00 a.m., just to keep me fresh until the cold early hours, when I often shoot off home behind the wheel of my XJ6 and crawl into bed.

A sudden single hard knock on the toilet door, and my breath rose in my chest.

Then I heard the muffled voice of Olivia.

'Dad! Is that you in there?'

I tried to reply, throat constricted with cocaine guilt. I cleared it loudly before answering, 'Shan't be a tick, sweetheart.'

'Oh, Dad! I'm bursting. Why can't you use your own loo?'

There was no way I could use our en-suite bathroom because Michelle and I never lock the door and I don't want her to know about my occasional cocaine hits.

I tore off a piece of loo roll, wiped the porcelain, screwed it into a ball and flushed it down the toilet bowl. Then I unlocked the door and came out to find Olivia scowling up at me. Although she was thirteen-going-on-fourteen, she still had an angelic face and showed no advance towards the stroppy teens. I gave her a lovably wide grin.

'It's all yours.'

'You and Mum have got your own. Why d'you have to use ours?'

This is territorial. My daughters think of the upstairs bathroom as exclusively theirs and, even when we have guests stay the night, I get the impression they would prefer them to use the downstairs loo.

'You were great tonight, Olivia. Brilliant dancing, sweetheart. You've improved in leaps and bounds,' I laughed. 'No pun intended.'

She frowned. 'You weren't bored?'

I placed a hand over my heart. 'I promise you, sweetheart, I loved every minute of it.'

Which was true. Although it was only a teenagers' part-time dancing school show, I genuinely enjoyed most of the evening – occasionally stifling a laugh when an overweight fourteen-year-old attempted energetic and acrobatic steps – but it was Olivia her proud parents were there to see and, although she was only in two dances out of twelve, I could see she was outstandingly good. And I don't think that's just a father's bias. I know she has talent, which is not so surprising seeing as her mother was a professional dancer before she met yours truly.

Olivia accepted the compliment with a serious nod before disappearing into the bathroom. I stood for a moment staring at the closed door, grinning like an idiot, swollen with pride and love. It lasted a microsecond before the drug kicked in an alert sensation, so that my brain could enjoy the sharp spark of decision.

Time to get the show on the road!

I hurried downstairs to one of my other pride and joys – the kitchen of my dreams from the pages of a glossy coffee-table book – super gleaming, comfortable yet functional, where the man of the house indulges in creating mouth-watering recipes. More than just a hobby, my passion is cooking. It keeps me sane and helps to keep the family well fed, even though I suspect that most of the time they're just humouring their old man with his gourmet indulgences.

Michelle sat at the enormous refectory table, a copy of *Heat* magazine in front of her, sipping a glass of her favourite pinot grigio as she watched the television that was perched on the far corner of the work surface. As I entered, I noticed her eyes darting in my direction before refocusing on the reality TV programme, a load of bollocks with some moron preening himself about converting an old shed into an elegant gazebo.

Although Michelle's glance had been split second, I could see it was enough to assess my appearance.

'You're wearing your extra-smart suit,' she observed without taking her eyes off the telly.

I grinned at her, and indulged for a moment in her appearance. Her short blonde hair with those delicate wisps that trailed invitingly along the back of her neck and her cute nose and those high, almost Eurasian, cheekbones and full lips and those baby-blue eyes. She was thirteen years younger than me, but she was still stunning and could have passed for late thirties. Easily. But then I'm biased, because I love my family. Including Jackie, my older daughter, who, at seventeen, is still in the terrible teens and often does impressions of Kevin and Perry.

I walked over to Michelle and kissed her neck, smelling her beautiful natural aroma of skin and sunshine. She was still suntanned from our recent family holiday in Cuba and I always marvel at how evenly and effortlessly she tans. Unlike me, who tends to go red and blotchy, which means I have to top the phizog up with a spray of aerosol amber.

As I moved away from Michelle, she picked up the remote and killed the trash on the telly. Her eyes were now trained on me, and it was a look I recognised as a search for truth. Her husband was about to go out all night and she wanted reassurance that it was all work and no play.

'Why your best lounge suit?' she asked. 'Shouldn't you be in your DJ?'

I sighed deliberately, showing her the frustration of having to explain yet again. 'Sweetheart, I supply the doormen. I employ the doormen. I'm in charge of the doormen. I only wear a dinner jacket when I have to deputise because of illness.'

'So what are you doing tonight?'

'I've got two new clubs to visit to drum up more business.'

A half-truth. Only one new club to visit, but I like to give the impression that my nights mooching around the clubs is not all play and no work. 'Plus,' I added for emphasis, 'I've got to go to the Liquid Velvet to give a pep talk to the boys after we had that fracas with the Yanks last week.'

'And that's going to take all night, is it?'

I jerked a thumb at the kitchen clock. 'Come on, Michelle. It's a quarter-to-ten now. By the time I drive to the West End and park, it'll be half-past. So don't wait up for me.'

She pouted and it was curiously attractive. I placed a hand over hers. 'I love you, Michelle. You're the only girl for me, sweetheart. You must know that.'

She shrugged. 'I do. It's just… '

'What?'

'I get lonely without you. You work such unsocial hours, and always on Friday and Saturday nights. I just wish we could spend more time together on the weekend.'

'They're the club's busiest nights, you know that.'

I felt the mobile in my pocket vibrate and heard its faint bleep. I fumbled in my jacket pocket and scanned the display. It was from Mal MacIntyre at the Kismet Club.

Shit! What did *he* want?

The message read: 'Ring me asap.'

'Fuck!' I complained, mainly for Michelle's benefit, so she could see I was a working guy with problems to sort out. 'What the hell does MacIntyre want?' I clicked to call back and told Michelle, 'Got an urgent call to make.'

It rang just twice before Mal picked up. 'Freddie Weston here. What's up?'

Mal's cracked and ageing voice had a whine to it that was irritating. 'Freddie, I'm up shit creek. It's Saturday night—'

'Yeah, I do know that, Mal,' I interrupted.

'—and I've only got one doorman out front. And I need two – minimum!'

'Fuck! Who's missing?'

'Fingers. He called me to say he had an urgent job come up.'

I raised my voice. 'Fuck him! Useless wanker!'

I caught Michelle's look of disapproval and turned away slightly. Mal MacIntyre went on to tell me that John Jolly, otherwise known as 'Fingers,' might be along later, depending on how his job went. I offered to pop down right away and deputise until he got there, and then hung up.

'Problems?' Michelle asked.

I stood up. 'Yeah. The Kismet Club's only got one doorman on tonight, so I'm going to have to fill in for John Jolly.'

She nodded at my suit. 'Shame, with you all done up for the West End.'

I detected slight triumph in her tone, as if she was pleased my night of PR enjoyment had been curtailed. Still, I couldn't blame her. She likes the reassurance that I do work, instead of gallivanting, and perhaps playing, away from home. Not that I do. Well, seldom do. It has been known on odd occasions, but that's purely a bloke thing, something men have done throughout the ages, since they were living in caves probably. But I'd never let it ruin our marriage.

'I'll try not to wake you when I get in,' I said, for the umpteenth time. 'I must dash.'

'You're not going to change into your DJ?'

'No time,' I said. 'I've got a black bow tie in the glove compartment. I'll stick that on.' I leant over and kissed her on the lips. 'I'll see you tomorrow.'

While I backed the Jag out of the garage, I thought about Fingers, wondering if he would show up later. It was fucking inconvenient, and there was always a chance the job could go wrong. Apart from being a club doorman, Fingers is a bone-breaker. For reasons of infidelity, gambling debts, or just mean-spiritedness, someone will hire Fingers to break someone's bones. The going rate is twenty-five notes per finger with a minimum of five fingers. And he'll do special rates, like all ten fingers and both arms for half a monkey.

John Jolly, aka Fingers, is a big geezer and well able to take care of himself, but he has to live with the knowledge that there is a law of averages and someone will eventually identify who was responsible for the excruciating pain of their snapped digits and go after him. I'd hate to be in his shoes when that day of reckoning happens.

I only hoped it wasn't on this particular night in May. As I drove round Wanstead Common, my mind became a clutter of violent thoughts, and I winced as I imagined the snapping back of fingers and thumbs and the agonising pain. I also knew that Fingers was like most men going off to a rewarding job, happy in his work. I could picture the scene.

★

The Last Dance pub was in a back street just off Mile End Road and Fingers stood squashed at the crowded bar sipping a large Bushmills. He would have preferred a pint but he didn't want to compromise the job by having to go for a piss. Although it was only ten o'clock and the pub would have an extension until one, he couldn't risk taking his eyes off his target, in case the bloke was on a crawl and decided to move to another pub. In fact, Fingers hoped he would, because then he could get the job done and get to the Kismet to earn a few more readies.

He could see the target at the end of the bar, a scumbag in a cheap denim jacket, greasy, lanky hair that looked as if he'd trimmed it himself when he was on a binge night out, and pock marks and acne glowing on his rodent-like features, which should have disappeared long before his fortieth birthday.

If Fingers ever felt sorry for his victims, it was a brief indulgence he flirted with until he thought about the money. He usually managed to justify the work by telling himself if he didn't do it there was always someone else who would. And when the victim looked like this arsehole – as useful as a fart in a spacesuit – then he obviously deserved what he had coming to him.

The arsehole glanced furtively over his shoulder, as if he had good reason to be nervous, and his eyes swept the bar for predators.

Fingers stared at him with fascination, wondering what his crime was. He looked like a grass. On the other hand, Fingers was intelligent enough not to judge on appearances. The client hadn't told him how the scumbag had flouted the unwritten law – sometimes it was best not to know – but as the client had paid for only the one hand, Fingers guessed it was probably a minor warning, otherwise this dickhead would be in traction for weeks.

Staring thoughtfully at his victim, Fingers suddenly became aware of their eyes meeting. He looked away casually and then dropped his head and stared into his whiskey, swirling it in the glass before he took a sip. He glanced casually at his watch, hoping that when he looked up and focused on his victim again the man would have thought nothing of it and would be scanning the rest of the pub for another source to fear.

But when he looked across to the other side of the bar, the scumbag was gone.

Shit!

Fingers knew he couldn't have gone to the bog because the Gents was on his side of the bar, so he must have slipped out into the night faster than greased lightning.

Fingers downed what was left of his Bushmills, slammed the glass on to the counter, squeezed his way through the crowd in the bar and exited hurriedly. He almost collided with three men standing in a cloud of tobacco smoke, mumbled an apology and a 'goodnight, gents,' and stepped forwards, looking both ways and wondering which way the arsehole had legged it. He couldn't see anyone in the dark street going away from Mile End Road towards a small estate of four-storey flats, so he guessed that his target would head for the sanctuary of the busy street where he would feel safe. Fingers hurried towards Mile End Road, glancing left and right when he got there. Apart from the heavy traffic zooming by, the pedestrian part of the road to his left was almost deserted; there was just one person he could see – a minicab driver getting out of his car and heading for a Chinese takeaway. From the right a gang of girls approached, giggling, shouting and swearing as they staggered and swayed in a line. But over the tops of their heads, he could just make out a scrawny figure, shoulders hunched, walking in the direction of Whitechapel. The bloke was less than fifty yards away, walking normally, feeling safe now he was on the main road.

Avoiding the inebriated gang of girls, Fingers set off after his quarry. He knew this area quite well, and he knew there would soon be a stretch of road where there were very few shops – and what shops there were would be long shut for the night. And, apart from the one he'd just come from, there wasn't another pub for a good quarter of a mile – maybe further. Fingers knew his target was heading for a stretch of road that was deserted and he remembered there was a bookie's about two hundred yards ahead, and right next to it was an alleyway.

He remembered the betting shop all right. He'd spent many hours in there, staring desperately at the TV screens along with all the other losers. Mug's game. Thank Christ he'd overcome the addiction and rarely placed a bet anymore. Now he spent more time pursuing the losers who'd done their shirt and owed the wrong person.

He put on a spurt, lessening the gap between him and his victim. He could see the man's lanky hair clearly now, and the grubby denim jacket. And, as certain animals can smell the fear of their prey, he could smell it on the retreating man as his intimidating footsteps increased their pace.

They were almost at the betting shop now. Fingers whipped a thin cigar from his inside pocket, held it close to his face and called out, ''Scuse me, mate!'

The man's fearful hesitation was fleeting before he pretended he hadn't heard and carried on, walking hurriedly.

Fingers ran after him and grabbed his shoulder.

'Hold up!' They were right by the alley now.

Nearly cringing with terror, the loser's head jerked 'round, staring into his tormenter's face, his fearful expression similar to a man in a horror film who has seen the monster from hell. But, disconcertingly, his tormentor smiled reassuringly.

'You got a light?'

'Sure.'

Hands shaking, the man fumbled in his jacket pocket and took out a Zippo lighter.

Fingers grabbed the man's wrist to steady his shaking hand, leant forwards and accepted the light, drawing on his cigar. He kept hold of the scumbag's wrist, took the cigar out of his mouth with his other hand, and stared closely and intimidatingly into the man's eyes.

'Left handed, are you?'

'What?'

'I asked if you was left handed.'

There was confusion and fear in the man's watery eyes. Fingers noticed a bus going by, followed by a taxi. Not that it mattered. It just looked like two blokes stopping to light up. And even if any of the bus or taxi passengers saw one man dragging another into an alleyway, what did it matter? It would be over in less than a minute.

Twisting the man's wrist in his grip, so that his Zippo lighter clattered on to the concrete, Fingers chucked his cigar and dragged him into the darkness of the alley. The man screamed, a sound not unlike the cry of a peacock, and he attempted to struggle, but resisting the pressure on his wrist was even more painful and the scream became a whimper.

'Please, mate,' he blubbered, 'I've got money – I can get you some. I'll make it worth your while.'

But Fingers had heard it all before. He clamped a meaty hand over the man's mouth and felt snot and saliva on his palm, a feeling that raised the anger in him, as though this was in some way the man's fault. At least four stone heavier, Fingers shoved the man to the ground, grabbed the roll of gaffer tape from his pocket, punched the man in the head a couple of times to keep him from struggling as he peeled and tore a strip of tape from the roll, and then gagged him. Now, all that could be heard was a frantic, desperate screaming through the plastic material, a high pitched squealing like an animal being slaughtered.

'Sorry, pal,' Fingers said in his most avuncular manner. 'Nothing personal. It's just a job. But it's your lucky night. Cheapskate only paid for one hand.'

Fingers straightened up, grabbed the man's left hand, yanking it upright, and snapped back the index finger. He was always surprised at how loud the clicks were, as if they were coming from a high-volume sound system. As he systematically bent back each finger in turn, saving the thumb until last, he chanted, 'This little piggy went to market…'

★

The Kismet Club was situated in the hinterland between Homerton and Hackney, sandwiched between a greasy doner kebab shop and a glamorous-sounding The Cutting Room, a drab building with the usual pictures of models in the window offering customers the delusion that an appointment will transform them into the stylish ideal of seductiveness.

Parking was not a problem seeing as most of the Saturday-night carousing went on less than a mile away in Hackney, and I soon found a space on a single yellow line not a stone's throw from the club.

The Kismet was once a rambling Victorian pub, a building that had seen better days. Its heyday as a club was in the seventies, but now it hangs on by the skin of its teeth and attracts a younger, rougher clientele, the sort of binge drinkers who like nothing better than to stagger out with a mouthful of obscenities, find some poor bastard to pick on, and get in the first punch so they can kick them to oblivion when they're down.

And that's just the girls!

As I approached the club, I could see Mario trying to keep order as a group of close-cropped lads queued to enter. For obvious reasons, bouncers work in pairs, and from a distance I clocked the worried tramlines on Mario's forehead and the insecurity of his body language as he tilted his head, allowing one yobbo in at a time but avoiding eye contact, still attempting the demeanour of a man in charge.

As I reached the entrance, he spotted me and raised a relieved hand in my direction. A homeless man appeared out of the shadows of The Cutting Room doorway and gave me the usual plea for some spare change.

The last yob to be let into the club turned and shouted, 'Fuck off and get a life, you arsehole.' I noticed he had a tattoo up the side of his right arm which read: 'I like fucking.'

Quality!

I probably would have given the homeless geezer some loose change, but the yobbo's obnoxious attitude boosted my generosity. I gave him a fiver and said, 'Don't waste it all on food.'

Shame. This was lost on the yobbo, who had already entered the Kismet and would by now be staggering towards the bar for a pint and a shot of something sweet and deadly.

'Thanks, mate,' the beggar said. 'I hope you have a good night.'

From the corner of my eye I saw him scuttle, crab-like, back to the shadows of his doorway. Mario gave me a relieved grin and I patted him on the shoulder.

'I've just got to have a quick word with Mal and then I'll give you a hand.'

'Thanks, Freddie. The rush starts in a half-hour and I don't like to work on my own.'

'It's OK, Mario,' I grinned. 'No need to call the union rep.'

Mario's face screwed into a puzzled frown and he ran a finger under the collar of his almost non-existent neck. I knew he was about to ask what I meant, so I patted his arm reassuringly and marched into the club. As I opened the door, the music hit me like a tidal wave, a pounding rap number, which would figure about ten thousand on my desert island disc list. I crossed the small dance floor, sticky with booze at the edges, and waved at Phil and Dave, the doormen who were on floor duty. The bar wasn't exactly crowded, and there were a few giggly girls, their voices sharp and shrill, sitting on chairs purchased when Thatcher ruled the waves – which was when the Kismet was last refurbished. The yobs were all lined up along the bar and I could hear language that would make Gordon Ramsey blush. No doubt Phil and Dave would be along to ask them to turn it down a bit, and then there would be a ruckus.

Jesus! What a shithole. Probably the worst club I have in my portfolio. But it was one of my first and I believe in loyalty. Besides, I liked the owner, Mal MacIntyre, and I knew he was going through a hard time at the club.

I gave Delbert, the resident DJ, a cursory wave, and went around behind his console to the door marked private and knocked loudly. I wouldn't have heard Mal's answer so I walked in. He was sitting behind a desk that was cluttered with paper – junk mostly – and a telephone. There was no computer because he told me he'd never got to grips with them.

He looked up as I entered and I caught the look of relief in his expression. He was sipping brandy from a tumbler and I could see he'd already chalked up quite a few, because he had that glassy, distant look in his eyes that indicated a desire to flake out on a sofa and forget his problems.

He was in his late fifties, thin faced with a hook nose, and was balding naturally but still hanging on to the grey hair at the back and sides. His suit, like the club, had seen better days, and on the collar of his open-neck shirt I could see how worn it was. The only evidence that he had tried to make the office presentable was a framed photograph of the Henry Cooper-Joe Bugner fight in 1971 next to a nudie calendar on the wall behind him. The rest of his cramped office was stacked with boxes of spirits and alcopops.

He put down his glass and gestured an apology with his hands.

'I know you got problems, Freddie, but I can't just leave it to Mario tonight. I've got to have two on the door – minimum.'

From the floor next to his chair, he raised a bottle of Spanish brandy, took another tumbler out of the desk drawer and poured me a generous slug.

I raised the glass and took a sip.

'I won't let you down. You know that. It's a bit quiet for a Saturday, though.'

Mal downswept his mouth and sighed. 'Yeah, Saturday's really fucked now. Everyone goes to Hackney. So now we're busier on Thursday's, even though we don't make nothing out of it. A tenner on the door and all you can drink until closing time.'

'Didn't you hear what the Minister of Health had to say about those sorts of promotions?'

'Fuck him! What does he know? The idea was to get regular punters in on Thursdays, and get them coming back on weekends. But it ain't fucking working. Bastards.'

I glanced at my watch. It was 10:15. Still too early for the Saturday punters who tended not to leave the pubs until half-past.

'The night is still young, Mal,' I said, trying to cheer him up. 'You usually get the punters in between half-past and midnight.'

'Not anymore,' he said, shaking his head. 'Not anymore.'

'You sound like fucking Eeyore.'

He gave me one of those looks, reminding me to bring him the Samaritans' number next time I visited. I decided to change the subject.

'How reliable is Fingers, usually?'

'Bit mouthy, punter looks at him the wrong way.'

'Apart from that?'

'He's OK. I reckon he must have a job on tonight.'

I laughed. 'Yeah, some poor bastard won't be able to...' I clicked my fingers, '...keep time to the music.'

Mal smiled weakly and sipped his drink. I could see that thoughtful distance in his eyes.

'Something bothering you, Mal?'

He stared into my eyes, and I could see the tortured resignation in his face, the sign of total defeat.

'Mark Lennox's outfit,' he said, waiting for my reaction. When I didn't respond, he went on. 'I'm being bled dry. Can't afford to pay my way. Turnover's high but there's very little profit. That's why I have to do these promotions.'

Mark Lennox. The name always gave me violent palpitations. I had a good reason to hate him but I'd never discovered why. I felt my nails digging into my palms.

'Lennox is an oily git,' I said. 'Bastard must have a free bus pass by now. I remember him coming to see my old man when I was ten years old...'

I broke off and swallowed the rest of the brandy. I didn't want to go there. Not until I'd got proof about Lennox and my father; and seeing as it happened forty-six years ago, that was not about to happen.

'You think Lennox was putting the squeeze on your old man?' Mal said.

I shook my head. 'For what? According to my mother and the rest of the family, my old man never had any financial problems. Just a hard worker who brought home the bacon each week.'

But the unanswered questions had plagued me all those years. Why did Lennox – who was still building his crooked little empire back in the late sixties – visit my old man that time? As far as I know, my father had never had any connections with villains. He was a docker, loading and unloading the ships down at East India Docks. So why would a young thug like Lennox visit my dad? And, more to the point, why did my old man commit suicide less than a week after Lennox met with him?'

Mal, noticing how I'd become preoccupied with troubled thoughts about my father, held the neck of the bottle over my tumbler. 'You want another?'

I placed a flattened hand over the rim. 'I won't thanks, Mal. The night is still young.'

Mal topped up his own glass and leant across the desk towards me, oozing sympathy and understanding. 'Look, Freddie, we all know Lennox had something to do with your old man's suicide…'

'Yeah, but what?'

Mal shrugged. 'Whatever it was, we might never know. But I'll tell you this, Freddie, Lennox will pay for what he's done. Not just to your old man, but everyone. What goes around comes around.'

I chuckled humourlessly. 'It's taking a bleeding long time then. I mean, Lennox is how old now?'

Mal didn't answer. He knew as well as I did that there is no divine retribution and the bad guys often die peacefully in their beds.

There was a knock on the door, followed by a blast of Ocean Colour Scene's 'Hundred Mile High City' as the door opened and Fingers entered wearing his DJ. He shut the door quickly to keep out the sound and stepped forwards, looming over Mal's desk like the Michelin Man.

'Sorry, Mal. I had a last minute assignment. Then I had to go back to my gaff to get changed.'

'At least you're here now, John, I won't ask what you been up to.' Mal laughed, rhythmically flexing the fingers of both hands.

Fingers watched the action expressionlessly. 'I'll go out front with Mario then,' he said, turning and lumbered out of the office.

After he was gone, I rose and said, 'Well, that lets me off the hook. I'd better shoot over to the Liquid Velvet. Adios, Mal. See you soon.'

'Yeah, take care, Freddie.'

As I let myself out, I could see by the way Mal was eyeing the brandy bottle that he would probably do the rest of it.

★

As I left the Kismet, the homeless geezer shuffled forwards. 'You've got my money, pal,' I said. 'Push off.'

He'd probably forgotten but he still scuttled obediently back to his doorway. I was about to cross the road to where I'd parked the car when I heard hurried footsteps behind me.

'Hold up, Freddie!'

It was Fingers.

'Can I have a quick word?'

Seeing the seriously polite expression on his face, I could guess what was coming, and I geared myself up for a confrontation.

'What's on your mind, John?'

'Liquid Velvet.'

'What about it?'

'You know me, Freddie. I'm a professional. I've never picked a fight with a punter…'

'No? What about New Year's Eve when a punter ended up with a broken wrist?'

'What? That Paki? Self-defence, weren't it? He had a go at me.'

'It was provocation, John. You called him a filthy raghead.'

'Yeah, well, it was after that bomb blast.'

I sighed loudly and deliberately, letting him know how pissed off I was. 'Look, John, I've got to push off. Can we cut to the chase?'

Fingers glanced contemptuously at the Kismet neon sign with its letter T blacked out. 'In a nutshell, Freddie, I'm sick of this shithole. *And* the wankers who come here. Liquid Velvet's more my style. I wouldn't mind working a club like that. Less aggro. Better class of customer.'

'And the celebs who are attracted by its upper-class vibes. It's funny, John, I never figured you for a star-fucker.'

I chuckled, knowing it would nark him. And it worked. I could see the resentment simmering, growing into a hatred which he struggled to keep in check. So I patted his arm playfully and gave him a reassuring grin.

'Tell you what, John, let me think about it. I'll see you later.'

As I turned and walked away, he said the one thing he must have known would wind me up.

'Us lot should stick together, Freddie. Don't let the coons take over.'

I wheeled around and caught the arrogant bastard's half smile. Immediate impulse: slam my fist into the fucker's face. But restraint was needed. Locking antlers with my staff outside the club was not a good idea. And not just for reasons of decorum. I know how to handle myself, but Fingers has a twenty-year advantage. Not only that, there'd be no Marquis of Queensbury rules if I decided to take the sadistic bastard on. But I wasn't going to take the cheeky fucker's comment lying down and contented myself with a tongue-lashing.

'If by "coon" you mean Jack, I've got all the time in the world for that geezer. So don't forget it. Guy's a diamond. One of the best. And he's got enough class to work somewhere like the Velvet.'

I couldn't resist that last little twist of the blade, and I walked hurriedly away, leaving the tosser to squirm over that one. As I got into my car, I could see him eyeing me from across the road, no doubt hoping for a time when the tables were turned.

Ignoring him, I drove past the Kismet and tried to put him out of my mind. But it wasn't the first time I'd heard a remark about Jack. Admittedly not outwardly racist like Fingers, but the snide comments can't disguise the jealousy and resentment because I have put Jack, who is Nigerian, in charge of one of London's most prestigious clubs. My number one doorman. Not that I give a stuff about what the others think. My choice. Besides, Jack is professional. Very black and very good looking, and although he is twenty-eight, he looks almost ten years younger. But he's really handy. Bright, personable and an expert at martial arts. And I like him.

Or was it that he reminded me of Angola back in the eighties and I was trying to atone, make up for the guilt and the dread I have felt over the years?

★

The West End was heaving and there was not a space to be had, so I had to park the Jag in the NCP at the top of Great Windmill Street, which would be an arm-and-a-leg jobby. Then I hurried through the back streets towards the alley between Upper Regent Street and Piccadilly where the restrained entrance to the Liquid Velvet fits discreetly between an up-market gentlemen's outfitter and a shop that sells mainly women's handbags that cost more than most people's monthly salaries.

The club rarely has problems, although it has been known for occasional football supporters to discover its whereabouts by accident after staggering 'round Soho pubs. Like I said, the Velvet's entrance is discreet, and the doorway, with its subtle brass name plaque, looks more like it might lead to a firm of solicitors than a night spot. Which is why we do not have doormen hanging around outside. Most of the Velvet's clientele know of its existence, and most of them can afford the steep prices. Liquid Velvet caters to successful footballers, their WAGs, politicians, actors, and of course celebs not known for anything other than their flimsy fame. Not to mention the fat-cat bankers and investment managers. We even get visiting American ex-presidents. It's that sort of club. So if any rat-arsed Millwall supporters try to blag their way into the inner sanctum of society's well-heeled playground they'll find themselves unceremoniously ejected by my handiest doormen.

I pushed open the door leading to the foyer and was greeted by Jack who interrupted his conversation with Melanie, the attractive receptionist who works two long weekend sessions to help her get through university.

'Hi, Freddie. I'm glad you could make it.'

Although Jack is Nigerian born and bred, there is little trace of a foreign accent, and I suspect he has worked hard at cultivating an English dialect, which makes him sound more third generation than a young Nigerian who can't have lived in London more than a dozen years.

Jack moved close to me and lowered his voice discreetly. 'I was a bit worried about you-know-who after the trouble we had the last time they were here.'

'I'm glad you raised those concerns,' I said. 'This is one gig I don't want to lose. Have our VIPs arrived yet?'

Jack shook his head. 'The night is young.'

'And they're definitely coming?'

'Yeah. They've booked a private room. And rumour has it that it's not just little treasure who'll be bopping tonight, but the ex-president himself.'

I glanced at my watch. It was 11:15. I had just enough time to get the other doormen together for a pep talk before the rush started.

'Right, it'll probably take off quite soon,' I said. 'Think you can cope on your own for ten minutes while I assemble the other lads for a quick word?'

'Sure, Freddie.'

I was about to turn away, and I noticed the hesitation, the look of concern as he opened his mouth to speak and then stopped.

'What is it, Jack?'

'I wanted to ask you something.'

'You want some time off.'

'How did you know?'

I sighed deliberately. 'Don't treat me like a moron, Jack.' Then smiled, to let him know I wasn't being difficult.

'Sorry,' he said. 'Only I've got some fight and stunt work on a picture.'

His eyes bored into mine, like he was a small boy and I was his father stopping him from going out for the evening.

'Good for you, Jack. But what's the problem? Why can't you do both?' I rubbed fingers and thumb together, gesture of the folding stuff. 'Double bubble.'

He shook his head, a worried expression still crowding his forehead. 'I wish I could. But they're night shoots. Wednesday to Friday. Plus Monday to Wednesday the following week. And if they get behind schedule...'

I thought about the Velvet's manager, Sean, and how difficult he could be sometimes over the smallest of problems. Jack must have seen the fleeting concern on my face and started to apologise again. I patted his arm reassuringly and gave him a disarming smile.

'Which Wednesday to Friday we talking about?'

'Not next week. The week after. I'm really sorry about this, Freddie.'

'At least you've given me a good deal of notice. And don't worry, I'll soon be asking for your autograph and you'll be able to buy this venue. So try not to worry about it. I just wish I had someone half as reliable as you to leave in charge.'

'I might be able to help there. I met someone at the gym. Says he's looking for a job. Asked if I'd put in a word for him.'

'Total stranger, is he?'

'Well, yeah. But he's good. Boxing and self-defence. Quiet bloke. Intelligent. He'd be worth meeting.'

'Where can I vet him?'

'He'll be at the gym tomorrow afternoon.'

'I'll see you there then. Right, I'd better have a word with the others.'

As I walked into the club, I heard Jack thanking me and I gave him a wave without looking back.

★

The staff changing room was better than most clubs I know and even featured a cosy three-seater leather settee which had been removed from one of the private rooms after it was deemed too wrinkled and worn to accommodate the club's more classy clientele. Along with a couple of folding director's chairs, these seats offered staff an opportunity to take the weight off their feet for five minutes. Not that the doormen had much time for a rest, other than the occasional quick fag breaks, which these days have to be taken outside – usually in the same area where we direct the customers through the emergency exit to a small courtyard out back which has an awning over the doorway as protection from the elements and is inaccessible to the public from the street because of the locked gates. In the event of an emergency the gates could be unlocked by the club staff.

With the exception of Jack, who I trusted to do the right thing, I had brought my doormen into the changing room for a quick briefing. And it would have to be quick, because the club would go into Saturday night overdrive pretty soon. I perched on a corner of the settee and prepared to address the troops.

Kevin, the oldest bouncer at thirty-five, had squeezed his oversized buttocks into one of the director chairs, which protesting with some squeaky groans, not helped by his nervous habit of moving a leg up and down rapidly from the ball of his foot.

Tony, the youngest doorman at twenty-three, leant against the corner of a grey metal filing cabinet, his eyes bright as he waited for me to start speaking. Almost too bright, I thought, wondering if he'd had a hit. But then, who was I to complain? People in glass houses, and all that.

Roger, in his late twenties, was ex-army, and stood with his hands behind his back, showing that he was paying attention, although the corner of his mouth always looked as if he was suppressing a sarcastic expression.

No point hanging about. I looked at my watch and got straight to the point. 'Tonight we have the return of our cousins from across the pond. And I do not want – I repeat – I do not want another fiasco like their last visit. Is that understood?'

I directed this question at Kevin, whose attention had already drifted and his moon-like features were surveying one of the blank white walls as if he was studying a Rembrandt.

'Kevin!' I prompted.

Kevin turned his gaze on me, his affronted expression implying that I was out of order in singling him out.

'It was provocation, Freddie,' he said with a shrug. 'Yankee fucker was effing and blinding all over the place.'

Roger snorted and caught Tony's eye. I ignored it and focused on Kevin. 'Since when have you been so prudish about the Anglo-Saxon, Kev?'

'Well, I could see he was upsetting the other customers.'

'Yeah, but you've got to be discreet. He was the president's cousin for Chrissakes.'

'*Ex-ex*-president,' Roger corrected me.

'He's still got a lot of clout,' I reminded him. 'And he was a lot better than Bush.'

Tony smirked and glanced at Roger. 'Even if he couldn't keep his Hampton in check,' he said.

Roger grinned back and shook his head. 'What about his daughter? She had a mouth on her that night.'

Tony's smile grew widely lascivious. 'You wouldn't kick her out of bed, Roger.'

'Don't be so sure. Her name's what puts me off.'

I felt I was losing control and snapped, 'What the fuck's that got to do with it?'

'Roger supports Fulham,' Tony explained.

Kevin gave a phlegmy laugh. 'See, Fulham and Chelsea are sworn enemies.'

I stood up and directed my aggravation at Kevin. 'Now look, her father's supposed to be with her tonight, so it's unlikely you'll get any bad behaviour. But just in case you do, I want total discretion. Is that clear? Any problems get Sean to smooth things over. Let him make the decisions.'

Kevin frowned. 'What if they behave like total prats, Freddie? What then?'

'Get Jack to handle it,' I said.

I noticed the shifty glances that passed between them and chose to ignore it. 'Revenge is sweet,' I said with a smile, took one of my business cards out, wrote a name and number on the back and handed it to Roger.

'Contact of mine at the *Daily Mail*.' A hack I knew, one of the few I tolerated. 'Just let him know they'll be leaving the club in an inebriated state and he'll send a photographer to capture the moment. Adios, amigos.'

As I opened the door, standing aside to let the three doormen out ahead of me, Roger stopped in the doorway, held up the business card, and tucked it into his pocket as he said, 'Why don't

I give your press guy a ring anyway? They're bound to be rat-arsed by the time they leave.'

I was about to object when he grinned and added, 'I guarantee it.'

★

After leaving the Liquid Velvet, I pushed my way across the frolicking crowds in Leicester Square and headed for Stringfellows. I checked out my staff at the door, had a vodka and tonic with Peter's brother, and then spent ten minutes watching a chinless hooray and two lap dancers. The arsehole must have been in his mid-thirties, at least – old enough to know better – and spending Papa's dosh, getting through twenties like there was no tomorrow. The two girls thought it was their birthday as they fluttered Bambi eyelids at the tosser, writhed, wriggled and wobbled their breasts, while he shoved money at them as if his life depended on it. His moronic, champagne-fuelled grin was trying desperately hard to show he was enjoying life to the fullest, but his bleary eyes were as vacant as a Blackpool B & B out of season, which started me on negative thoughts about the meaning of life. So I upped and left.

I walked up Charing Cross Road to Tottenham Court Road and went into The Sportsman, had a quick flutter at the blackjack table and came away with a bullseye. Not bad earnings, fifty quid for ten minutes work. Not that I do the casinos that often. But every now and then, like when I feel lucky, I'll have a little punt. And I never go chasing my tail. If I'd lost fifty I would have come away and written it off as part of life's rich.

The next club I visited, Viva La Trash, on the north side of Oxford Street close to Charlotte Street, was pounding away when I arrived. One of my doormen let me in, and I headed for the bar. I bought myself a bottle of San Miguel and tried to see if there was anyone I knew in the place. I spotted Vanessa Feltz with a group of people at a corner table. I caught her eye and she smiled and waved a greeting. On the bar stool next to me, a dark, short-haired man sat with his back to the bar, staring at the dance floor, eyeing up the single women. I recognised him as a villain from a recent TV drama series about Manchester gun crime. I toasted him with my beer and told him how much I'd enjoyed his series, but he just nodded an acknowledgement and wiped me off his radar as if I'd crawled out from under the proverbial.

Yeah and fuck you! I thought. And I would have verbalised it but I have a reputation for keeping it businesslike and professional. Instead, seeing as time was marching on, and it was now sliding up to 2:00 a.m., I perked myself up with a line in the Gents before moving on to the next establishment, which was Jax on Kingley Street, now under new management. The owner was a guy called Phil, Cardiff born and bred, and nicknamed 'Phil the Greek' because of his distinct resemblance to a younger Duke of Edinburgh. His was the club I was targeting as my next client. But, as we sat at the bar, shouting to be heard, Phil protested with continental shrugs and gestures that he wanted to keep his hiring decisions in-house. I knew this was just a strategy to keep my costs low, so I made an arrangement to meet him in two weeks' time and moved on to another two clubs. The last was my favourite, a little basement dive just off Golden Square, which was a drinking club, pure and simple, where you came to hear yourself speak and play the odd game of poker or brag. What in the good old days would have been called a spieler.

It was just coming up to four o'clock and most of the clientele had drifted off in an early morning haze to literally flop into bed. Except for a nine-card brag school of ex-villains, who had now turned old and grey and had book publishing deals going and were pitting their skills against a couple of actors from *EastEnders*. It was a perfect marriage, villains and showbiz, showbiz and villains. Nobody would care who lost or won, it was the rubbing shoulders in a manly way that counted. I did a quick mental shufty of how much booze I'd consumed and it came to four large vodkas, bottle of premium beer, and a slug of cheap Spanish brandy at the Kismet. I risked one more pint of lager, normal strength. And that was me done for the night. But first I visited a little late night greasy spoon I know for breakfast – a sausage sarnie and a mug of instant. Then, as I walked back to the car park, I chewed a tablet of Airwaves chewing gum to take the smell of the alcohol away.

When I got to the NCP I knew I'd still be over the limit, but I'm a fair sized bloke and I can hold my liquor. But just to be on the safe side I got the sure-fire prop out of the glove compartment.

No copper's going to stop a chauffeur in a Jag at 4:30 on a Sunday morning and the hat always works. And just to prove it, a cop car pulled alongside me at the lights at Cambridge Circus. I gave them a friendly nod – not overdone – and they turned right to head south along Charing Cross Road.

Always works.

When I got home I crept into bed beside Michelle and felt her stir and turn away from me in her sleep. As soon as my head touched the pillow, sleep was instant.

The air around us fizzed with bullets that ricocheted off the rocks. Two hundred savage faces and only thirty of us. Outnumbered. Not that it mattered. We were highly trained. And they were stuck down there on the road, hampered by all their equipment. From high above we slaughtered them. They couldn't come after us because of the mines we'd laid. One poor bastard ran forwards and the explosion took his leg clean off. He lay there screaming until my mate, Bill, put him out of his misery. Yanks call it a turkey shoot, and we picked them off one by one, every single round counting. We were the professionals and they were the poor fuckers who'd been forced to fight for some corrupt cause. But in this situation it was either us or them.

A few of them got away. Good third maybe, their vehicles skidding off in panic. Only one of our blokes had been hit, and that was a stray bullet that ricocheted off one of the rocks. No great damage. A flesh wound, which Bill attended to. We walked cautiously and carefully down to the road, avoiding the mines we'd planted, to inspect the damage. I stood over one of the dead, the one next to the abandoned armoured car, the one I knew I'd shot clean through the heart. It was like I'd been kicked in the bollocks. Fuck me! That face! He couldn't have been more than twelve or thirteen. He was still a child and his black face had sweetness and innocence in death, like he was just sleeping.

Time was suspended. Shocked and devastated by my kill, I stood over his corpse fighting back tears. I knew this was the end. I couldn't do this anymore.

The cacophony roused me from a drugged sleep and a nightmare, but I realised I had already been stirring and the nightmare was real. It was my memory and conscience. Hard to avoid. And the disturbing, screeching noise, like a soundtrack, added to the nightmare, a horrific reminder of my past.

I sat bolt upright and looked around the bedroom. Michelle was not beside me. I felt nauseous, either from my guilty past or too much booze. Or maybe it was that terrible thumping noise, punching inside my head. At last I placed it. Pounding, scratching and screeching coming from Jackie's room.

I leapt out of bed. This was all I needed on a Sunday morning after a night of heavy toil.

2
BLOW JOB

'Jackie! Jackie!' I yelled as I pushed open her bedroom door. 'Turn it down will you?'

She couldn't have heard me above the din but she caught sight of me from the corner of her eye and looked startled. With a skidding screech she brought the record on the console to an abrupt halt. I always wondered how come these vinyl records getting scratched didn't get scratched, if you know what I mean. But that's technology for you. Can't expect an old geezer like me to understand. Give me Sinatra or Tony Bennett any day.

Jackie's expression segued from startled fawn to angry feline. 'Dad! You don't just walk in. Try knocking, will you?'

I tried to make light of it, gave her a cheeky grin, shrug of shoulders and exaggerated Jewish gesture. 'You can hear me knocking above that racket?'

'I had a great sound going. I was recording it, and you've fucking ruined it.'

'Oy!' I objected. 'You're not so old I can't wash your mouth out with soap.'

Her jaw jutted out, like a fighter offering a challenge. 'Just try it.'

'Isn't there a volume control on that thing?' I said.

'Well, of course there is.'

'So why not use it? Why do we all have to suffer?'

'It's not the same with the volume turned down. It's...'

She struggled to find the right word.

'Quieter?' I offered.

'Dad, you just wouldn't understand.'

I sighed deeply. It was a familiar, no-win situation. Trying a different tack, I adopted a helpless expression and rubbed my forehead.

'Please, Jackie, I've had a difficult night. And I've got the start of a headache. Just turn it down a notch for me, would you? Or better still, use the headphones.'

She glared at me, our eyes locked in a standoff. Eventually she capitulated, grabbed the headphones and plugged them into the console.

'Satisfied?' she snapped.

Allowing her to have the last word, I watched for a moment as she began spinning the turntable and fiddling with the dials. Her anger was channelled into whatever sounds she was creating and her body language was aggressive as she attacked the record deck, glaring down at it, thoroughly involved, giving it some punishment.

I left her to it and went to get showered and dressed. I had yet to face Michelle and tell her I needed to meet Jack's contact at the gym and Sunday lunch would have to be postponed until late afternoon.

★

Michelle was in the garden, giving it a final tidy-up before the sad grey weather spread its doom and gloom over our metropolis. I told her about my meeting at the gym and she accepted it without so much as a token objection. Obviously she had something else on her mind and I guessed the reason.

'What's up with Jackie recently?' I said. 'It's like living under a volcano. She seems permanently angry about something and it's getting worse.'

Michelle shrugged, bent over to tug at a gnarled root poking out from under the azalea bush and said, 'Teenagers! Who'd have them?'

Her reply was feeble considering the way I knew she was feeling about our daughter and I wondered if she was hoping it was a passing phase and any day now our Jackie would be transformed from teenage beast into a more mature and devoted daughter.

Yeah, right!

I glanced up at Jackie's bedroom window, which overlooks the back garden. Since I'd asked her to plug in the headphones all was quiet, but I could still hear the cacophony in my head, sending me into a deranged spin.

'And this scratching of records,' I complained. 'Scratching records! I ask you! It's driving me round the twist.'

Michelle straightened up and gave me one of those looks. *You wouldn't understand. You're too old.*

'It's part of her course, Freddie.'

I nodded grudgingly. Jackie was doing two years of music technology at college and we were grateful she had found something she wanted to do since her GCSE results had been average and A-levels were not an option. But deep down I was disappointed and I wanted more for my first born.

'Jesus!' I grumbled. 'Music technology. Why couldn't she have picked something quiet, like – er – painting or something?'

'Because painting doesn't give you the opportunity to work with rock bands,' Michelle said.

'And that's the only reason she chose it?'

'What do you think?'

I sighed and glanced at my watch. 'I think I'd better head for the gym. The sooner I go, the sooner I come back.'

I gave Michelle a parting kiss and she said, 'I'll pick your mother up at half-twelve. Oh, by the way, Sandy phoned. She and Ian can't make it. She's got a streaming cold.'

'Oh great! And I haven't seen my big sister for a couple of months.'

'She can't help it if she's got a cold, Freddie.'

'True.'

'We'll have dinner about half-three if you can make it back by then.'

'No problem,' I said. 'You know how much I value a family dinner on Sunday.'

Michelle's mouth twitched. 'And Jackie won't be joining us.'

'Oh? Why's that?'

'She said she's off out with some of her mates.'

'You'd think one day a week she might make an effort for us all to be together as a family.'

Michelle gave me a crooked smile. 'At least we won't have to put up with the sulky expression. It puts you off your food.'

'There is that,' I replied and turned towards the garage, giving Michelle a backwards wave. 'Be as quick as I can.'

★

The gymnasium was near New Cross in South London. It took me longer to get there than I expected. The Sunday traffic was heavy, with the usual family outings for retail therapy – or trauma, depending on how the kids behaved – and crossing under the Thames at the Blackwall Tunnel was slow going as one lane was closed for roadwork.

Egon's Boxing Club and Gymnasium is just around the corner from New Cross Gate underground station and it took me over an hour to get there. By the time I'd found somewhere legal to park and looked at my watch, it was getting on for two. I had half an hour to check Jack's potential doorman out, then I needed to get back for Sunday dinner.

Jack had left word at reception that I was visiting, and I signed the book and walked 'round the cavernous gym to look for him. The ceiling of the building was arched, as if it might once have been some sort of hangar that housed light aircraft, the walls were metallic grey with functional pipes deliberately exposed and painted rather than concealed, giving the venue a high-tech character that went with the gleam of shiny boxing gloves and keep-fit equipment. I had been here once before to meet Jack. It must have been on a weekday because I don't remember it being this crowded. The place was heaving with testosterone, and the sounds of focused puffing and punching echoed around the space, coupled with the squeak of rubber trainers deflecting and dodging. Looking up at one of the three boxing rings I saw two ultra slim females kick boxing, their faces masks of concentration. The other two rings were busy with men sparring and taking instruction from staff trainers.

The gym was ethnically diverse – every nationality seemed to be represented under this roof – and because everyone was dressed in similar exercise gear, it was difficult to focus on Jack. I eventually spotted him on a training bike and sidled up to him. His ebony body gleamed with sweat and he didn't notice me until I spoke and pointed to his distance meter.

'Only 15.6 miles. Call that exercise?'

He stopped pedalling, blew the sweat from his upper lip and smiled. 'This is just a warm-up.'

Small talk out of the way, I cut to the chase. 'So what do you know about this geezer you recommended?'

'About his background you mean?' Jack cast his eyes up at the roof as he thought about this. 'Nothing much. He spent his childhood in London, then his folks moved north – to Liverpool.'

I could feel my instinctive suspicion rising to the surface. 'And you believe him, Jack?'

Jack shrugged, got off the exercise bike and mopped his face with a towel as he spoke. 'Who knows? Maybe he's been a long term guest of Her Majesty's government. So what? A lot of your boys have been in trouble with the law at one time or another.'

'Yeah, but I like to know who I'm dealing with. Introduce me. I'll check him out.'

'Sure. Follow me.'

Jack led the way to a far corner of the gym where a young, fit-looking man was giving a punchbag a good seeing to. Jack tapped him on the shoulder and he reacted quickly, spinning round as if he was ready for action. When he saw it was Jack, he relaxed and dropped his gloved hands to his sides.

Jack introduced us. 'Bob, I'd like you to meet Freddie Weston. Freddie, this is Bob Hughes.'

Hughes held up his boxing gloves by way of an apology. 'Good to meet you, Mr Weston. Sorry, can't shake hands.'

'First names, Bob,' I told him. 'Call me Freddie.'

He threw me a cheeky grin. 'Cheers, Freddie.'

My first impressions were positive. OK, he had the usual close-cropped hair, morphing his head into a bullet shape, but didn't all the young men these days? He had one discreet tattoo that looked like a small dragon on the top of his left arm. Bulging biceps. This bloke pumped iron regularly. At a rough guess I would have put his age at late twenties, early thirties maybe. He looked like most young blokes these days, just one of life's young clones, someone whose identity you'd be hard pressed to recall. Except for one distinguishing feature – on his right cheek was a small jagged scar, evidence that he could have been attacked with a broken bottle, maybe in a pub fight. Not a good sign, but with my background, who was I to criticize? But what impressed me were his eyes. Dark brown, lively and passionate, which held my gaze with an energy that showed he was a determined young geezer.

'Jack tells me you're looking for a job,' I said. 'And he's given you a very good reference.'

He shrugged modestly. 'Well, I like to keep myself fit.'

'It's not just a question of how well you can handle yourself, Bob. I need someone reliable, someone who can deputise for Jack. You ever worked as a bouncer before?'

'I did a stint in a Scouse club once.'

'How long ago?'

'Six months.'

'Why d'you pack it in?'

Bob Hughes hesitated, looked down at his boxing gloves, then looked me in the eye before replying. 'During the day I was supplementing my income by taking what didn't belong to me. I got two years at Walton for burglary.'

'Thanks for being honest. How long ago was this?'

'It was recent. That's why I decided to come back down south.'

'Has Jack told you anything about the Velvet?'

'He told me they get some pretty well-heeled customers there. And some of them can be right tossers. So you gotta be careful about how you handle a situation.'

'Exactly. How good are you at stopping a ruck?'

Bob gave me a confident grin. 'Diplomacy's my middle name.'

We were interrupted by a shout from the nearest boxing ring. 'Hey, Bob! You're next, mate.'

I glanced over to where a coach stood in the ring, raising the ropes to let out the previous fighter, and was now waving Bob over. Bob gave me a gesture of regret by turning over his gloves and he started to apologize.

'Sorry, Freddie, I'm next on—'

'No, go on, son,' I interrupted. 'I'd like to see how you make out. I'll catch you later.'

His eyes flashed and he grinned warmly. 'Yeah. Cheers, Freddie!'

As I watched him climb into the ring, Jack asked me what I thought.

'Seems a bright enough bloke,' I said.

'He don't strike me as a bullshitter, either,' Jack said with a tone of pride, as if Bob Hughes was his protégé.

As I watched Hughes starting to dance around his opponent and I thought about that scar, I turned to Jack and said, 'One thing don't seem right – his folks heading up north, where the grass definitely ain't greener.'

Jack frowned thoughtfully. 'Could be all kinds of reasons.'

'Yeah, like his old man wanted to move to a high unemployment area.'

'You got doubts, Freddie?'

I shook my head. 'Maybe I'm being paranoid. But I'd hate to lose the Velvet. If that happened, and word got about... Goodbye West End, hello East End.'

'Jesus, Freddie! I feel scared to recommend him.'

I patted Jack's arm reassuringly. 'My decision at the end of the day. Don't feel responsible, compadre.'

'All I can say is, from what I've seen, I've been impressed. *Really* impressed. The guy does kendo, judo, karate – you name it. I can't see him beating the shit out of a customer, if that's what you're worried about, Freddie.'

I glanced over at the ring, watching Hughes ducking and dodging, light on his feet and sure with his punches. 'Boxes well,' I said. 'Look at him move. Fred Astaire of the boxing ring. Wonder why he's not taken it up as a career?'

'Maybe the time he spent in Walton put paid to it.'

'Yeah, could be.' I glanced at my watch. It was almost half-two. I told Jack I'd have a serious think about Bob Hughes and text him with my decision. Then I left hurriedly to get back in time for our family dinner. Just as I reached the car my mobile bleeped. It was a text message from Michelle.

'Be warned yr mum says its yr dads birthday. C u l8er M x.'

Shit! That was all I needed, my mother hitting the gin and getting maudlin over Dad as if it was only yesterday.

As I headed through Greenwich towards the Blackwall Tunnel, I thought about Mum and how Dad's suicide had affected her. For years after his death she hit the bottle, and it was left to Sandy to nurture me through the terrible teens. She must have done a good job because I came through them relatively unscathed and maybe caring for my grieving mother had something to do with it. Then, as time passed, Mum's drinking levelled out and she forgot about the pain of my old man's death. But now she's older, the problems seem to have returned, as if it happened only yesterday. I try to be sympathetic but I could have done without her gin-soaked emotions on what should have been a relaxing family Sunday.

A BMW cut me off, and I narrowly missed hitting it as the driver squeezed the car through a narrow gap between my Jag and a traffic island. I would have tooted angrily but I was too busy thinking about Mum bending Michelle's ear over Dad's death more than forty years ago. I could picture the scene.

*

Freddie's mother, Janet, was like a tiny sparrow, dwarfed by the large kitchen table, leaning on one bony elbow, staring into her gin and tonic while Michelle opened the oven door to check on the roast potatoes. They had both made the usual small talk and eventually ran out – mainly because Michelle was aware of her mother-in-law's melancholic mood and knew the old lady was getting nearer the subject of her husband's suicide. Satisfied that the potatoes and leg of lamb were almost ready to dish up, she slammed the oven door, turned the heat down, and got herself a glass of pinot from the fridge.

Freddie's mother raised her glass in a toast, glad they were now complicit in their boozing. 'You've changed your mind then.'

'On a Sunday the yardarm starts earlier, Janet.'

Janet laughed. 'I'll drink to that. Would there be any more gin to go with this tonic?'

Michelle shook her head disapprovingly but it was half-hearted, part of a double-act they always went through when Janet came over and started on the gin. She fetched the gin bottle from the work surface and refilled her mother-in-law's glass.

'I don't know why you bother with the tonic.'

'I like to taste the gin. The tonic just puts a bit of fizz into it.'

Michelle busied herself by turning the gas down on the hob, hoping the vegetables were not going to be over-cooked. She avoided eye contact with Janet, preferring to make small domestic actions designed to ward off the inevitable subject of Freddie's long dead father.

Dead for well over forty years, and still the old bat wouldn't let it go.

As if Janet could sense what she was thinking, she said, 'There are some things you never get over. I suppose it's because you have questions but no answers.'

Michelle decided to ignore it. 'Look at the time! God knows where Freddie's got to. He was only going to the gym.'

'Blimey! Keep fit! That doesn't sound like my Freddie.'

Michelle congratulated herself for deflecting the subject from Freddie's father. 'To meet someone,' she explained.

'Cheers!' said Janet. Then: 'And happy birthday, Charlie.'

In spite of her reluctance to involve herself in this hackneyed subject, Michelle found herself saying, 'Even after all these years you still remember his birthday.'

She could have kicked herself. Now Janet would be up and running.

'I loved him,' Janet sniffed loudly and took a slurp of gin.

Michelle wondered if the sniff was border tearfulness or merely some sort of catarrh.

'I suppose I still love him,' Janet continued. 'And I keep asking myself why. It's more than forty years ago, but there's not a week goes by when I don't think about it. Why would a man avoid going to work one day and then hang himself from…'

There was a long pause. Michelle took a sip of wine and thought about the suicide. She wanted to say, 'Freddie thinks there was a reason and it was all to do with that gangster Lennox.' But whatever the reason, Michelle had always secretly thought of the suicide as a selfish act, and now she thought she would hint at her true feelings and let Janet glimpse by implication the way she felt about the pointless death of Freddie's father.

'Didn't it ever make you angry? I mean, Freddie was ten when it happened. Sandy was fourteen. I know if Freddie did something like that to me and the girls…'

She let the accusation hang, unfinished. But Janet missed the suggestion of blame against her husband.

'I never once felt angry,' she said. 'If there'd been a reason – money difficulties or something – then I might've felt differently. But to do something like that, he must have had a screw loose… he must have… to do a thing like that. Freddie's convinced there was a reason. He thinks that Lennox had something to do with it.'

This was not what Michelle wanted to hear. She knew about Freddie's suspicions and prayed he would never find the proof he needed. Although Lennox was at least seventy, he was still an ugly force to be feared, and controlled a mob of loathsome villains. If Freddie ever found out the truth about Lennox and the relationship between him and his father, she knew he was capable of wreaking the most terrible revenge on the gangster. And that would open the flood gates and jeopardise the safety of their family.

She walked over to Janet and gently placed a hand on her thin wrist. 'Listen, Janet, would you do me a favour? Don't talk about this to Freddie. It's only opening old wounds. Let's have dinner without mentioning something that happened more than forty years ago. Without constant reminders, Freddie's happy to give Lennox a wide berth. Best way.'

'Bit difficult to ignore Charlie's death, what with it being his birthday. Freddie'll know by the date.'

Michelle sighed with irritation and moved back to the hob. 'He was only ten, Janet. I doubt if he'd remember his father's birthday if it wasn't for you reminding him.'

They heard a key in the front door, followed by Freddie calling out, 'I'm back!'

Michelle spun round from the hob and stared pleadingly at her mother-in-law. 'Please, Janet.'

'OK,' Janet said. 'I promise I'll keep shtum about it.'

But the way her mother-in-law shrugged after she spoke, Michelle doubted her promise was genuine. Especially if she had a few more gins.

★

As soon as I entered the kitchen I could tell Michelle and Mum had been talking about Dad. And the guilty look on Mum's face told me she'd been warned off the subject. Well, that suited me fine. Even though I'd like to get that bastard Lennox for whatever part he played in my old man's death, there are times when I'd like the past to disappear and never rear its head again. But it's always niggling, always in the back of my mind, like someone probing into my brain with a metal instrument. When you don't have reasons, it can sometimes drive you insane. With knowing comes closure. Then again, maybe not. Perhaps with knowing comes revenge. Inevitable. So let's not go down that route, I told myself. I was determined to get through this Sunday dinner, enjoying my family and living with both feet firmly rooted in the present.

I went and gave Mum a kiss on her cheek. She reeked of gin. 'Blimey, Mum! How many have you had?'

'This is only my second.'

I exchanged a look with Michelle who flashed me an ironic smile.

'Yeah,' I said. 'Only the second treble. Jesus, Mum! I wish you'd go easy on that stuff.'

'Don't nag, boy,' she said as I went over to the hob and kissed Michelle.

'Freddie, would you mind dishing out the dinner?' Michelle asked. 'It's all ready.'

I frowned. 'Why? Where are you going?'

I saw the warning signal in her eyes, indicating that she had a tactic of some sort. I realised what it was when she said, 'To get Olivia down for dinner. And afterwards we can show Janet our holiday snaps. I'll go and get them. They're in Jackie's room.'

I gave her a conspiratorial smile. Holiday photos! Anything to keep Mum off the morbid forty-year-old suicide routine.

'Good idea,' I said.

As soon as she left I picked up the oven gloves, pulled open the oven door as a sizzling hot sweet smell of lamb and rosemary blasted the air, sending a plume of smoke up towards the extractor.

'You know it's your father's birthday today,' Mum said.

Ignoring her, I said, 'Smells good.'

But she wasn't going to let it go.

'Did you hear me, son?'

As I took the meat and potatoes out of the oven, I raised my voice slightly, letting her know that now was not the time for bitter memories. 'Jesus, Mum! It's all so long ago. Just forget it, will you? At least while we're having dinner.'

But, as usual, she was like a dog worrying a bone long after it's been picked clean.

'It's funny, I can't remember what I was doing a week ago, or who I spoke to, or where I've been. But I can remember the day I found him quite clearly, like it happened only yesterday.'

I turned from my dishing-up chores and gave her a faint, pleading smile. 'Please can we talk about it later, Mum? And not in front of Olivia while we're having dinner.'

'OK.' She made a zipping gesture across her mouth then smiled. 'I'm looking forward to seeing your holiday snaps.'

Relieved, I chuckled. 'Even Jackie managed to smile in one or two photos.'

While we were having dinner, Olivia chatted away to her Nan about school and her dancing triumphs. And her grandmother managed to keep off the subject of Dad and his birthday. But it was now Michelle's mood that worried me. Since she had gone upstairs to fetch Olivia and collected the huge bundle of holiday photos, she had lapsed into a silence which at first I interpreted as a deep sulk, but then I realised that something was seriously bothering her. She hardly said two words throughout dinner, other than trivial statements to do with the meal. In fact, if it hadn't been for Olivia and her grandmother chatting away, the bad vibes that Michelle was creating would soon have everyone dumb and depressed.

Fortunately, Mum and Olivia were oblivious to Michelle's frame of mind. For the moment, at least.

As soon as our pudding – a summer pudding made by yours truly – had been eaten, Michelle stood up and handed Olivia the bundle of snapshots.

'Darling, would you like to show Nan the holiday photos while I take your Dad and show him the disgusting state of Jackie's room?'

'The state of her room!' I said. 'Tell me something I don't know.'

But there was a fierce look in her eyes, signalling something important she wanted to tell me.

'I'd like you to come up and look at it, Freddie.'

Olivia, her antennae suddenly alert and sensing something strictly confidential was going on between us, stopped talking to Mum.

'Her room's always a tip. What's the big secret?'

Michelle snapped with frustration. 'It's worse than normal. And I'm fed up with it. Olivia, just show Nan the photos while I show your Dad Jackie's room.'

Olivia shrugged hugely, as if to say what's the big deal, and I followed Michelle upstairs to Jackie's bedroom. It was untidy, but I'd seen worse, and I said so to Michelle but she ignored me and led me over to Jackie's desk, where our daughter's diary lay open.

'I know I shouldn't have read it. But the photos were next to it and it happened to be open at that page.'

She watched me as I read the diary entry, my stomach starting to feel queasy as sickening images burst into my brain. I tried to push them away, but they intruded like a repulsive porno film. My daughter, for Chrissakes! This was my seventeen-year-old baby. Eventually, when I'd read the sickening account of her lust, I looked at Michelle, tears in my eyes, my voice trembling with both desperation and rage.

'Jesus Christ! This is disgusting. I can't believe she'd do such a thing.'

Michelle's tone was hard and brittle. 'When I read it I felt sick to my stomach.'

'It's our daughter for fuck's sake!' I spat out, trying not to shout in case Olivia heard me. 'Our daughter. A fucking slag.'

Michelle looked as if she'd been slapped. 'Freddie! Don't! Calling her… that… won't help.'

'I know what I'm reading, Michelle. And it's disgusting. She's a fucking slag.'

'She's a groupie, Freddie. They've been around for years.'

I stared at the diary entry again, my eyes wide with disbelief and horror. 'Jesus Christ! Not only did she give this guitarist a blow job, she did it in the communal dressing room in front of the rest of the group. How could she? The dirty little slag.'

'Freddie! We must get this into perspective. When you were that age, didn't you ever…'

'Don't give me that double standards and hypocrisy bullshit,' I cut in. 'It won't wash. She's my little girl, Michelle, and I don't know how I'll feel about her anymore. Sucking some guy's cock in front of a load of other blokes, for fuck's sake. I wish I'd never read about it. I'd have been happier in my ignorance.'

'Wouldn't we all. But it's not her fault, Freddie.'

'No? Seems to me she was more than willing to—'

Michelle stopped me with a hand on my arm. 'That guy in the group used the fact that she was besotted by him. He used the power he had over her. He took advantage and abused her. But that's not what upset her.'

Michelle stared at me, waiting for me to cue her.

'Go on,' I obliged, though I desperately wanted to bury my head and escape from my daughter's dirty secrets.

'In the diary entry on the next page… she went back the next day for the second performance. And he turned her away. Refused to see her.'

'Bastard!' I hissed, my fists clenching, imagining them pounding into a young bloke's face. 'Treating her like cheap shit.'

I stared into Michelle's eyes and we both felt the pain of my words. That was when I started to crumple and my eyes filled with tears. Michelle came forward and held me in a close embrace.

'She's our little girl, Michelle.'

We held each other tight, frozen in our despair, my tears wet against her warm cheeks. But if there was any comfort to be had, it was from the sweet smell of revenge. 'And anyone who hurts one of our girls will pay the price,' I whispered.

I felt Michelle's body stiffen and she drew away from me, her eyes boring into mine. 'What are you going to do?'

'At least we know this wanker's name, and the name of his group. It's there in the diary.'

Michelle's face was like tightly stretched parchment. 'Freddie! I don't want you to do anything stupid.'

'Oh, don't worry,' I told her. 'I'm not going to harm a hair on his head. But I know a man who will.'

3

LIFE IS CHEAP

I'll never forget that Sunday. After I'd run Mum home, I got back to our place about 8:00 p.m. Jackie was home and I've never felt so awkward in my life. The silences stretched uncomfortably, followed by stilted, polite talk and sly, sidelong glances from Michelle and me, observing our daughter, our imaginations running riot with scenes I definitely didn't wish to picture.

About 9:30 Jackie went up to her room, as did Olivia, leaving Michelle and me to stare at a television drama without taking it in. By now I'd done at least half a bottle of Glenmorangie malt in just over an hour, and what with the emotional upheaval and everything, my eyes were starting to feel heavy. We talked some more about Jackie and the guitarist, Michelle trying to persuade me that we had to come to terms with our daughter's sexuality and how would it have been if I'd been seventeen and invited for sex with a girl band...

I conceded that she had a point, but still secretly plotted revenge.

Monday morning I ran Olivia to school and then Jackie to college. I kept staring in the car mirror at Jackie, examining her face like a specimen under a microscope. She caught my eye several times and, sensing my hostility, shouted angrily, 'What! What's wrong?' I mumbled that there was nothing wrong and avoided staring at her after that and was relieved when I dropped her off, glad I could distance myself from the heavy atmosphere. But I still wasn't going to let it rest. Closure. That's what was needed. And revenge meant closure. Then we could all get on with life.

★

Wednesday. Usually a fairly quiet night at the Kismet, but without Fingers and no one else to deputise, I had to put in some time as a doorman. I was all done up in my monkey suit when I called on Mal in his seedy cubby hole to find out what had happened to Fingers.

Flushed of face, hands shaking, Mal tilted the glass of brandy to his lips as I entered.

'Wotcher, Mal,' I said. 'I'd go easy on the sauce if I were you. Another drink-driving ban and it'll be a custodial sentence next time.'

'That's a bow tie you're wearing, not a dog collar. Shut up and join me.'

So saying, he got another glass out and poured me a healthy slug. Once we'd toasted each other, he stared at me, waiting, knowing I was dying to cash in on the details.

'So what happened?'

'What goes around,' Mal replied, a triumphant, told-you-so glint in his eye, but it could have been the booze. 'Fingers got his comeuppance at last. Sorry to see him go, but he's broken one bone too many. It had to happen. Just a question of time.'

'Inconvenient,' I sniffed. 'Care to fill me in on the details.'

Mal licked his lips in anticipation of a good story. 'When he left here last Saturday night, he decided to walk home. He'd done that on Monday as well. Fat bastard was probably trying to lose some weight. Nobody knows whether he was followed. It's tricky following someone in a car if they're walking. It's more likely someone followed him on foot after he left here on Monday, then waited for him last night as he took his usual short cut across that small industrial estate near where he lives.' Mal sniggered and corrected himself. 'Lived. It was the perfect place to do someone. No one around at that time of night. No houses. Nothing but small factory units.'

'So how did he meet his end?'

'Wheels. Hit and run job.'

Mal paused, allowing me time to take it in.

I took a large gulp of brandy as I thought about the end of Fingers. Walking home along an isolated road. The road to nowhere. Lonely footsteps. Suddenly... out of the dark... headlights. The roar of an engine. The end in sight. I could picture the scene.

★

The Range Rover, stolen only two hours ago and probably wouldn't be missed for a while, was parked outside a small unit dealing in air conditioning maintenance. Off the road, next to a white van, in the shadows of the unit, on an incline leading to the building's entrance, the four-by-four waited in darkened silence. The atmosphere inside the vehicle was tense but there was also a feverish excitement that both men found difficult to keep in check. Not by anything that was said. In fact, they hardly spoke. The mood came from their heavy breathing, and the way they exhaled air every so often, trying to calm down, knowing they were about to commit the ultimate crime.

The driver was barely out of his teens and this was to be his test. It wasn't so much the money, the ton he was getting for the hit; it was more a rite of passage, a coming of age as a gold medal killer. An initiation ceremony and a test for no one but himself. Taking it to the brink. Once this was done, there was no going back. You'll be a man, my son.

In the passenger seat, wearing the same scruffy denim jacket, and reeking of sweat, cigarette smoke and a diet of greasy food, his hair as unwashed and as lanky as the night he'd been followed from The Last Dance pub along Mile End Road, sat the architect of the revenge killing. He would have preferred to do the job himself, enjoying the cock-stiffening ecstasy of accelerating and grinding the fucker's bones into the road. The trouble was, his left hand was in plaster and was still giving him grief. But it wasn't just the injured hand that kept him from whacking the fucker himself.

Employing the kid for the hit gave him a feeling of power. It was what the head honcho did, king of the rackets.

He and the kid were gasping for a fag but didn't dare light up. There was only about one hundred yards of road until it curved along the estate, and just before the bend there was an alley which was where their target was headed. So if he spotted cigarettes glowing in the Rover, and then heard the motor start up, the fucker could make it in a mad dash to the alley.

'Fuck me!' the kid complained. 'What if he gets a cab home tonight? We been waiting half an hour now. I need a fucking smoke.'

'Look, shut it. Smoking's bad for your fucking health.'

The kid snorted with laughter. 'Not as bad as being hit by a motor like this.'

To show he was a good sport, and to keep the kid sweet, his conspirator chuckled. Then suddenly hissed a warning as he spotted a dark figure walking down the road towards them.

'I think this might be him,' he whispered. 'Yes, it's him. No mistaking the fat fucker. Wait till he gets level with us then switch on and go for him.'

'Headlights?'

'Yeah, let the cunt know he's fucked.'

They waited as their target hurried along the deserted road. As he drew level with the aircon company, the kid turned the ignition key, pressed hard on the accelerator and the engine roared to life. Startled, Fingers froze. It took him a moment to realise what was happening, especially as the headlights suddenly caught him in their beam. Running flat out for his life, he knew he couldn't possibly make the alley before the Range Rover caught up with him. But the futile realisation came too late and he hadn't covered more than five or six yards when he was caught in the back and thrown sideways high in the air. He landed with an agonising smack against a brick wall leading to the alley. He lay on his back, helpless, his body twisted in pain. He saw the violent flare of the brake lights as the Range Rover screeched to a halt in front of him. And he screamed and begged for his life as he saw the reverse lights come on. His tormented scream was cut short as the rear offside wheel smashed his head into the wall with a sickening crunch. The scream was the last thing he heard echoing through his brain.

The Range Rover U-turned and, tyres squealing, headed back towards the main road. The man in the denim jacket, his heart pumping, clenched his right hand into a fist and raised it as if his team had just scored.

'Yes! Did you see that fat fucker trying to run? Like a helpless fucking rabbit. Nice one, son.'

The kid nodded but said nothing. He was thinking about his initiation into this other world that he now inhabited.

As they drove along the main road, the man in denim told him to take the next turning and pull over. Knowing the back offside lights would be smashed, he was shrewd enough to know he needed to dump the vehicle as soon as possible in case the police pulled them over.

Once they had turned into a side street, the kid stopped the car, cut the engine and turned expectantly towards his accomplice. The man in denim fumbled with his right hand in his breast pocket and pulled out four twenty pound notes.

'Listen,' he said, 'I've only got eighty. I know I promised you a ton, but I'll catch you at the weekend for the other twenty. Right?'

There was a pause while the kid considered this. Then he said, 'No problem, mate. And if you need any more work done, you know where to find me.'

The man in denim slapped him on the leg as he started to get out. 'Sure, son, be glad to give you a reference any time.'

★

I needed to get front of house and join Mario on the door but Mal was clearly in a talkative mood and poured us another drink.

'Don't worry, Freddie,' he assured me. 'Mario can cope for a little while.'

'Something on your mind, Mal?'

He tried to conceal a smile and I knew he had gossip to impart.

'I don't suppose you'll be attending Fingers' funeral.'

'What makes you say that?'

'Family connections. I only found out recently who Fingers' old woman is. Bird by the name of Barbara – Babs – O'Brien.'

I shook my head. 'Means nothing to me. Should it?'

'She's Mark Lennox's niece. So the Lennox mob'll be at the funeral. Guaranteed.'

He waited, watching carefully for my reaction. I sipped my drink, taking my time before answering. 'Mal, I never had much time for Fingers and I had no intention of attending his funeral. But now you've told me about the Lennox connection, wild horses wouldn't keep from paying my respects.'

Mal grinned. 'You watch yourself, Freddie. Lennox might be getting on in years, but he still controls a tasty mob of arseholes.'

'I'll bear it in mind.' I let out a long sigh, letting Mal know there was something else. 'It was fucking inconsiderate of Fingers to get himself topped just when I had need of his services.'

Mal raised his eyebrows questioningly, waiting for me to elaborate.

'Sorry,' I said. 'I need to keep it under wraps. But, offhand, you know of anyone in the same line of business as Fingers?'

He shook his head. 'I'm trying to mix with a better class of person. What about some of your old mercenary or army pals?'

'We were in the 9th Squadron Para Engineers. We were the elite, Mal. Be a bit like asking Frank Lampard to play for Hereford United.'

'Question of pride, is it?'

'Something like that.'

★

A week later I was sitting at the back of a chapel of rest in a crematorium near Barking. I could have sat a bit further up the front as there were loads of empty pews but, understandably, because of Fingers' chosen line of work, the service wasn't that well attended and most of the mourners were spread out across the front two rows, sitting with spaces between each other, trying to make the turn out look better attended than it was. Most successful villains usually merit the treatment – the plumed horses pulling the hearse slowly through the East End, with more flowers than the Netherlands can export. But this was Fingers, a feral untrustworthy arsehole who would turn on you if the price was right. Presumably the only reason Lennox and his men were attending the funeral was because of his niece, who I discovered a few days before the event was his older brother Nick's daughter. Nick Lennox had been shot fifteen years ago in a Billericay pub, his killer had never been caught and his brother Mark showed his loyalty by lending his support to the daughter, even though she had shacked up with a toe-rag like Fingers.

In the second row I spotted him, Mark Lennox, hair too uniformly black for someone his age, cut to medium length and tapered neatly at the back, sitting next to his henchman, Mickey 'Machete'Whiting, and a few other suited-and-booted villains with whom I was thankfully not acquainted. In front of Lennox sat a blonde woman, who turned her tubby, heavily made-up face to one side and dabbed at a tear. A dutiful gesture for the deceased. This I guessed was Fingers' other half and Lennox's niece. Her uncle leant forward solicitously and patted her shoulder.

The chaplain, a decrepit old geezer with a long pointed nose that wouldn't have looked out of place with a dewdrop hanging off it, consulted a scrap of notebook paper, giving a few facts (lies) about John Jolly's colourful past, his 'sense of adventure' – I saw Lennox turn to Mickey Whiting, whisper something in his ear and smirk – and then the chaplain peered closely at the paper, and adjusted his half-moon glasses. His voice droned an apology about John Jolly's sorry misdemeanour when he was sent down for three years at Wormwood Scrubs, became a model prisoner, and absolved himself of his crimes by helping young prisoners to go straight after their release. After a few more lies about him being a popular pillar of the community and other such clichés, the chaplain suddenly ducked his head and muttered – as if he wanted to get this farce over and done with as quickly as possible – a brief prayer commending the departed to sit in peace with the Lord in heaven.

I tried to picture the scene but it was too bizarre to visualise.

And then - don't know how I kept a straight face – booming out of the sound system as the coffin began its journey to the flames, Frank Sinatra singing 'My Way.' It always brings tears to sentimental villains' eyes. Soon Fingers' body would be consumed and I wondered what Barbara O'Brien would do with the ashes. Maybe her uncle had some sentimental ideas about the disposal, scattering them off Southend Pier. It's the sort of schmaltzy gesture that appeals to East End villains. Me, I think, what's the point? When you're dead, you're dead, so you're not going to worry about where they scatter your ashes. Might as well be flushed down the bog, far as I'm concerned.

As I was at the back row of the chapel I was first to leave and hung around outside, waiting to face Lennox. I hadn't seen the gangster for a good twenty years and I wanted to confront him. Don't ask me why. I don't know. Maybe it was because I wanted to get close up to him and read the guilt in his eyes. The last time I'd seen him was at a boxing match and even in the distance separating us I could tell he knew that I held him responsible for my old man's death and time would not heal the retribution I craved.

First out was Mickey Whiting, raising surprised eyebrows when he saw me. Face like a potato with add-on features, broad shoulders and curly ginger hair. Actually, I don't mind Mickey. I've seen him around on his own in a few clubs. I know he has a reputation and has cut more than a few people in his time, but he's always been all right with me. I take as I find. And I did hear that Lennox once ordered Mickey to give someone a Chelsea smile and Mickey threw up afterwards.

'Hello, Mickey,' I greeted him cheerfully. 'How's tricks?'

He acknowledged my greeting with a grave nod, saying nothing. Either it was respect for the bereaved – which I doubted – or he had never met me in the company of his boss and didn't want to demonstrate any matey-ness towards me.

The grieving widow followed closely behind him, being comforted by her uncle. When he saw me he stopped and removed his arm from around her shoulders.

'Well, well, well,' he said. 'Long time no see. I didn't expect to see you here.'

He looked frail, his complexion sallow. Not a healthy specimen and maybe not long for this world. But I didn't want him to die just yet. I was still searching for answers.

He was astute enough not to offer his hand, avoiding the humiliation of a refusal to shake it. As we stared at each other I could tell he knew I was aware that something went on between him and my old man all those years ago. Lennox would have been a young tearaway in his mid-twenties then, and my father was a docker. I'd often thought that my father had perhaps got involved in nicking loads of dodgy cargo. Nicking was rife in those days until the imports were packed into containers, and even then it was not unknown for an entire container to go missing.

After a pause, with our eyes locked in combat, I said, 'I thought I'd pay my respects. Seeing as John was one of my occasional employees. That's when he wasn't working freelance for himself.'

Through gritted teeth, Lennox said, 'Yeah, he told me you employed him at the Kismet.' He smiled suddenly, though there was no warmth in his eyes. 'Which I suppose makes you one of *my* employees.'

'Oh? Why's that?'

He smirked, and I wanted to punch that wrinkled face with its downswept mouth. And that ridiculous dyed hair that looked like syrup wound me up.

He turned to include the widow in the conversation but I knew it was directed at me. 'I don't think you know Freddie Weston. He supplies the doormen for many London clubs, including the Kismet where John worked. And as I have the lion's share in the club, I suppose indirectly Freddie works for me.'

The atmosphere was electric and all the mourners who had by now gathered round could sense the tension.

'I didn't know you had controlling interest,' I said.

'Soon will have. And then it's goodbye MacIntyre.'

'Yeah, Mal did say something about being… finding it hard to make ends meet.'

A cold smile from Lennox, a snake uncoiling. 'So when I do take over we must talk about renewing your contract with the club.'

'Maybe,' I said, diverting my attention to Barbara 'Babs' O'Brien. 'Sorry about your loss. It was a nice service.' I kept my voice level, not wanting it to sound like too much of a piss take. 'Whose idea was the Frank Sinatra song? Nice touch.'

'Better than that "Jerusalem" shit,' Lennox growled.

'Don't tell me you chose it?'

'What if I did?'

I shrugged and gave Babs a sympathetic smile. 'So what will you do with his ashes? Any plans?'

'Fuck knows,' she replied. I saw Lennox wince and one of the acolytes stifled a smile.

But I was warming to my subject now. 'Did you see that film with Bob Hoskins and Michael Caine, where they take the ashes down to Margate? I know Fingers – sorry! – John had a few fond memories of Southend. Maybe you could all have a ceremony on the pier and scatter him there.'

Lennox suddenly boiled over with anger and, forgetting where he was, snarled, 'You taking the fucking piss?'

Protesting innocence, I turned over my palms with a shrug. 'No, I swear. I just thought John's other half might want a few suggestions what to do with him… his remains. No one wants the urn on their mantelpiece. Bit morbid that.'

'We wasn't married,' Babs broke in. 'Not legally, any rate. But it would be nice to scatter him.' She appealed to Lennox. 'Maybe Freddie's got a point. We spent many a happy day down Southend. The pier's a good suggestion.'

I saw Lennox's jaw tense. 'Shit fucking suggestion, darling.'

'But why, Mark? We could drive down for the day and stroll along to the end of the pier…'

'No fucking way, Babs!'

'But why not, Mark? Why not?'

Lennox stared coldly at me. Now look what you've started. I smiled back.

'I expect he has his reasons,' I said, making it obvious he was being small-minded for no good reason.

'But I don't understand why not,' Babs wittered.

'I just can't stand piers,' Lennox snapped.

'Mark's got this – what's it called? – aquaphobia?' Mickey explained. 'He's scared of water.'

Lennox rounded on his henchman. 'Who the fuck asked you?'

'I was just trying to explain to Babs…'

'Well, don't! Fucking shut it!'

Mickey's gormless expression made him appear more simple than normal.

Other mourners were starting to arrive for the next service and I could see the shocked expressions on their faces.

'Time we left for the wake,' Lennox snapped. He stared at me. 'I don't suppose you're coming back for a drink.'

I shook my head. 'Got a busy day ahead.' He turned to leave and I added sarcastically, 'But thanks for the inviting offer.'

He stopped and threw me a poisonous look before disappearing, followed by his entourage. As the next mourners began to assemble, some of them glared at me accusingly, as if I'd been the one using bad language.

I strolled slowly to the car park, not wanting to catch up with Lennox's mob. I thought about the futility of my attending the funeral, doing it simply to stir things up between us. What had I hoped to gain by it? There was no way the gangster was ever going to admit to what went on between my father and him all those years ago. He'd probably take the truth into the grave with him.

And, from the way he looked, the grim reaper was already sharpening his scythe. But his was one funeral I wouldn't be attending. No way. Unless, of course, instead of a cremation they decided to bury him. That might alter things. I might go along just so I could piss on his grave.

4
BOTTLE SCAR

When I got home after the funeral, Michelle was sitting at the kitchen table drinking coffee, a scrap of notebook paper in front of her. When she looked up with that frown of accusation I knew so well, right away I knew what was written on the paper.

'I was about to send an e-mail,' she said, 'and I found this list on your desk.'

I could have kicked myself for leaving it lying around. Caught bang to rights. No sense denying it now.

'Their tour dates,' I shrugged. 'I got it off their website.'

'I didn't realise you were into that sort of music.'

'I'm not. It's one particular guitarist who interests me.'

'Don't do it, Freddie. It's not worth it.'

'I don't know what you're talking about.'

'Yes, you do. You're planning to use one of your boys to rough him up.'

I gave her a disarming smile and spread my arms out. 'OK, I'll come clean. That was the general idea.'

She sighed with frustration and shook her head. 'After we read Jackie's diary, and you made that threat, I wanted you to take revenge on the bastard. I really did. But the more I think about it, the more scary it seems. Forget it, Freddie.'

'So what made you change your mind?'

'I don't want you becoming involved in anything violent. It looks as if this group is going places; they're getting quite well known. If anything happens to this guitarist the police'll become involved.

And it'll probably be in all the papers. You could end up in jail, for God's sake.'

'Yeah well, don't worry your pretty little head about it.' I followed my sexist remark with a laugh to show her I was joking.

'Freddie!' Her voice rising, the volcano about to erupt. 'It's not funny. It could...'

I raised a placatory hand. 'Seriously, Michelle. It's all off. The bastard's been let off the hook. Bloke I had in mind to do the job's out of commission. It's his funeral I've just been to.'

'So that's it then?'

I nodded. 'You sound disappointed.'

'I suppose I am in a way. I wanted him to suffer for what he'd done. On the other hand, the other part of me wants to move on and forget it.'

'You're right,' I lied. 'Let's forget about it.'

No. There was no way I was going to allow that bastard to get away with what he did to Jackie. My mind was already buzzing with other potential avenues of revenge.

★

I hadn't seen my old mate Bill Turner for at least three months and I felt guilty. He was going through a hard time financially and I was about to approach him with a dubious proposition knowing full well he needed the money and would find it hard to turn down.

Bill lives in Shepherd's Bush, just off Goldhawk Road, so I found a multi-storey car park close to the green and walked the short distance to his place and what is euphemistically called a studio flat. Not a bad area, having become gentrified over the years and most of the Edwardian houses are now distinctly des res, especially as the district is within cab-hailing distance from the West End. His flat's on the top floor of a three-storey building in a tree-lined street with residents' parking – at a price. I pressed the buzzer for his flat. After a moment the intercom crackled and his grizzled voice asked, 'Who is it?'

'It's me, chaps – Biggles,' I said in a BBC voice.

Without replying, he pressed the buzzer and I pushed open the door. The hall was awash with junk mail and pizza delivery leaflets. I took two steps at a time up the six flights of stairs and found Bill waiting for me on the landing at the top. It was the only flat on the top floor, an extra storey built into the roof, and even though Bill is a mere five foot five, he still had to stoop slightly. That was the thing about Bill, he was tougher than most soldiers I had ever known and people often made the mistake – to their cost – of underestimating him. Wiry, but all muscle, with a boyish face that never seems to age, close-cropped dark hair, and smooth darkish skin that suggests Celtic or Roman ancestry.

As I reached the landing, I had to duck and twist my head uncomfortably.

'I think I recognise the face,' Bill said, peering up at me in the gloom. 'Of course, now I remember. Freddie Weston.'

'Yeah, sorry, mate. I know it's been a while but…'

I couldn't think of an excuse, so I entered the flat, relieved to be able to stand erect as his room was in the centre of the roof. At least he had a separate kitchen and bathroom, and the combined living room and bedroom was reasonably spacious; but living in one room would drive me round the twist. Bill doesn't seem to mind, and likes being within tube and taxi distance of where it all happens.

I glanced around the room to see if anything had changed since my last visit and clocked what looked like a pristine computer work station, squeezed uncomfortably close to the end of his double bed, which had to be a fairly new acquisition. As did the Toshiba laptop on it.

'Didn't know you were computer literate,' I said as he shut the flat door.

'I'm learning,' he replied. 'Want some fire water? Seeing me hesitate, he added reassuringly, 'Courvoisier.'

'Be rude not to.'

'And I'll make some coffee to wash it down.'

I shook my head. 'Not for me, mate.'

'I'm making fresh, you snobby git. In a *cafetière*.'

I gave him a wide grin. 'You've twisted my arm. So how's life been treating you?'

'Like a shit sandwich.'

'No change there, then. Seriously, mate, what you up to?'

Bill glanced at the laptop. 'Writing my memoirs. Well... trying to. All those diaries I kept when we were mercenaries... I was going through them... and some of the exploits... well, we got in some pretty tight spots. I thought it'd make a great book.'

I didn't say anything and followed him as he limped towards the small galley kitchen. The limp was a souvenir of Namibia, when his Jeep hit a landmine. He spent two months in an American hospital, while they repaired his leg with steel pins, piecing it together like broken china. I stood in the doorway watching while he got the brandy out of the cupboard. He poured two generous measures, handed me one and we clinked glasses. We both took a slug and then he switched the kettle on and started to prepare the coffee.

'The trouble is,' he said, continuing a thought, 'it's not easy, Freddie.'

He saw me frowning, and explained, 'The writing. I mean, I don't know a verb from an adjective.'

I shrugged and took another swig of my brandy. 'I wouldn't worry about it. Most of the major villains who do the rounds of the clubs these days are calling themselves writers. But they don't do much of the craft. They just tell their story and other writers do the donkey work.'

'So how do they go about it?'

'I don't know. I'll ask around, see if anyone can point me in the right direction. I'll start with Jock Panton. He's just got a publishing deal.'

Bill frowned as he spooned Continental Blend into the cafetière. 'Name rings a bell. Remind me.'

'The Butcher of Limehouse.'

'Oh yeah. Jesus! If he starts telling tales, won't a few villains get a bit brutal? I mean, isn't there some sort of *omertá* code they have to observe?'

'Nah. He'll probably make most of it up. They all do. The publishers and the public lap it up. In the meantime, how you earning a crust?'

'I'm not. Got debts piling up. Using one credit card to pay off another. At this rate I'll end up selling *Big Issue*.'

I nodded thoughtfully, biding my time, waiting to hit him with my proposition. He finished making the coffee, watching me warily out of the corner of his eye, and probably sensed I had something on my mind.

I moved aside for him as he carried coffee and mugs on a tray into his main room. He placed them on a square coffee table and gestured for me to flop into his only comfortable easy chair, while he opened a black metal folding chair, sat and poured the coffee. As I moved towards the easy chair, I glanced at the Word document on his laptop screen, which had the bold title **Chapter Four. The Angolan Fiasco**.

I had an uneasy feeling about this, even if his ambition to write his autobiography went nowhere. But just in case it did, I would have to have a word about what he intended writing in that fourth chapter, which was a worry. But first things first.

As soon as the coffee was poured, I said, 'Fancy doing some work for me?'

His eyes narrowed as he peered at me suspiciously, but with a twinkle of amusement from the self-knowledge that he already had me sussed.

'So that's why you're here. Bit short staffed, are you? I hope I'm not your last resort, Freddie.'

I turned my palms up and shrugged an apology. 'Sorry, Bill. I know I haven't seen you in weeks…'

'Months,' he corrected me.

'Yeah, all right – months. I won't leave it so long next time. Promise.'

'So what's the job? Not another club.'

'Sorry, Bill, I haven't got any new clients yet. And you know I can't use you in any of my existing clubs; not after that fracas at Rupert's. Small world, mate. Word gets about. Them's the rules. You know that.'

Bill gave a loud impatient sigh. 'Get to the point, Freddie. What's the job?'

'Little trip to Manchester. No more than one night away. And I'll pay you a grand plus your expenses.'

'Good money for a night's work. Must be double-dodgy, this one.'

I knew it was time to cut to the chase.

'I just want you to break some bloke's fingers. Someone who's been a bit of a naughty boy.'

'Who's the target? A villain?'

I shook my head. 'Guitarist who plays in a band. Been putting himself about with the young girls.'

I hadn't noticed before just how quiet it was up here in the roof, with no traffic noises from the street below. Now the silence was accentuated by the gears grinding in Bill's head as he thought about my proposition, but his face was impossible to read. He stood up suddenly.

'I think I could do with another top-up.'

I watched as he limped to the kitchen. He seemed to have aged considerably, and I thought maybe he wasn't the right bloke for the job. Perhaps I was wrong to even consider asking him. When he'd collected the Courvoisier, he stood for a moment in the kitchen doorway and shook his head.

'You're not interested then,' I said.

'In a nutshell, Freddie.'

He came and sat down, and poured us two more cognacs.

'Reason?' I asked him. I could guess the answer but I needed to hear him say it.

'I'm not getting any younger, mate. Even so, if it was a stunt like we used to get up to in the old days – fair enough – I might still be up for it. I mean, what we did back then was not strictly illegal. Most of the time MI6 and the Foreign Office knew what was going on and chose to ignore it. But stalking a civilian and breaking his fingers… well… it ain't exactly…'

'Cricket?' I suggested. 'But the bastard deserves it, Bill.'

'I expect he does. But I'm not your man. Sorry, mate.'

I gave him an understanding smile. 'Question of pride?'

'Maybe,' he mumbled as he took a sip of brandy.

'I had you figured right then.'

He lowered his glass and stared at me with a puzzled frown. 'If you knew I'd say no, what made you ask?'

'Had to give my best shot. And I know you could do with the folding stuff.'

Bill pointed a finger at me. 'Now if you'd told me the target was Mark Lennox, I might have reconsidered your offer.'

'You don't even know Lennox.'

'So what? You told me he was responsible for your old man killing himself. That's good enough for me.'

I smiled at Bill. 'Thanks for your support.' The smile disappeared as I stared into my brandy, adding, 'Actually, I've just seen Lennox at the funeral of one of my employees.' I looked up and caught Bill's puzzled expression and told him about the funeral and the meeting with Lennox.

'So,' he said at the end of it, 'if you know the bastard was blackmailing your old man, and was responsible for his death, what's to stop you from taking a pop at him?'

'Suspecting is one thing, knowing is another. OK, deep down I just know he was responsible, but I need more than that. I need reasons. And it's stupid, I know, for years I've never really thought about Lennox, and tucked my old man's suicide away to somewhere safe in the back of my mind. Didn't really think about it. But, for some reason, it seems more important now.'

'Could it be,' Bill began, staring into the distance as he examined his thoughts, 'that now Lennox is aging fast, you're scared you'll end up never knowing the reason your dad killed himself?'

I toasted Bill with my cognac before swallowing a mouthful. A smooth and burning swell in my chest and my voice grated in my throat when I spoke. 'In a nutshell, mate.' Echoing his words of just a moment ago, I felt embarrassed, but he appeared not to notice, and frowned thoughtfully as he considered my predicament.

'So what you gonna do about it?'

I shrugged. 'I don't know. What *can* I do? I know Mum feels the same as me. And the older she gets, the more obsessed she becomes, talking about his death as if it happened yesterday. It ain't healthy, Bill. I know I've got to let it go, but seeing the bastard again brought it all back to me. But I might have to face up to the fact that I will never know the truth.'

Raising his eyebrows and shaking his head sympathetically, he said, 'Sorry, mate, I know it's always going to plague you, and I wish I could suggest something but… so tell me about Manchester job. What's that all about?'

I sighed deeply. 'Oh, I don't know, Bill. I think I might give it the elbow.'

'Can't have been that important.'

'Maybe it wasn't, in the great scheme of things.'

To change the subject, I asked him if he had any plans.

He pursed his lips, tilting his head to one side as he thought about this. 'Well, I suppose I might see if I can find someone interested in reading about my crazy life.' He chuckled. 'Remember that temporary work we did at that film studio in Battersea. That was one hell of a crack.'

I laughed. 'Yeah, I often get pictures of the dwarf screaming with fear as he flew towards the rafters. I've dined out on that one.'

This was just before the Angolan escapade, while we were waiting to be recruited. We heard on the grapevine that someone needed a couple of geezers to do some general carpentry and building work in a small film studio shooting a commercial. It was a three day shoot – I can't even remember the product now – and it involved a Boeing 707 having its wings blown off, with a young child actor dressed as Superman zooming up to rescue the plane. The large model aircraft, about fifteen feet long, stood vertically on its tail and was supported by a scaffold rig, and a scaffold pole through the centre of its fuselage. It looked the business. Gantries were set up either side of the plane for the cameras, dry-ice machines to give cloud effects, and wind machines to blow the dry-ice across, and a winch took the child actor – whom Bill had christened "the dwarf" – hurtling towards the plane. But the director was not pleased with his special effects and explosives expert, who provided a big-bang effect but little in the way of spectacular visuals. The director wanted flames and firestorms, not the damp squib the so-called expert was giving him. Which was where we came in. The director heard that we were mercenaries and knew about explosives. He came over, asked us for our credentials, and we assured him that we were ex-Paras from a specialist unit and our job was the disposal and delousing of booby traps and bombs in Northern Ireland and we were trained in all explosives and IEDs. He seemed satisfied with that and we did a deal for more money, but only if we succeeded in giving him the visual effects he so desperately needed. We then went to the nearest shop and bought ten boxes of Swan Vestas matches, bags of sugar and tinfoil. The special effects man looked on with growing suspicion as we filled the tinfoil with this lethal mix of sugar and match-heads, wrapped up in strands of toilet paper. Eyes boggling with horror, the effects man wired up the charges ready for detonation, and we warned the studio to stand well back. As soon as the director shouted "action", there was a mighty explosion, flames shot out of the back of the fuselage, which split in half as the plane was jerked upwards. One of the wings was torn off like a page being pulled out of a notebook, and hurtled across the studio where it smashed into the toilet door. Flames shot out of the jagged hole left by the wing, and the child actor screamed with terror as he was winched towards this destruction. Bill and I were helpless with laughter, and although the director suspected us of doing it for a lark, he didn't seem to care. He got his shot.

'Yeah, that would make one hell of a story,' I told Bill, 'if you tell it right. But if you should get a bite for this book, there's something I want you to do. Something that's bothering me.'

Bill stopped smiling at the memory and frowned. 'Oh? What's that?'

'I want you to keep me out of your book.'

'Jesus, Freddie! You kidding? We had so many escapades together, that might be a bit tricky.'

'I'm serious. I don't ever want Michelle to find out about those boy soldiers in Angola, and the reason I packed it in.'

He nodded gravely, and I could see the memory of the slaughter running through his brain. 'Sure, Freddie, I still get pangs of guilt about that one. I might leave it out...'

I nodded towards the laptop, which had now gone into its temporary shutdown mode. 'Only I couldn't help noticing when I came in, you've reached a chapter about Angola.'

'There were loads of capers in Angola, not just... that one.'

I noticed his voice fading at the end of the sentence, as if afraid to mention the battle which resulted in my temporary breakdown.

'I know,' I said after a pause. 'But just in case you decide to unload your guilt onto paper, like loads of people searching for redemption do...'

He interrupted me with a raised hand. 'I promise, Freddie. If I do feel a need to unburden myself, you'll be given another name, mate. A completely different identity.'

'Thanks,' I said. 'Much appreciated.' I felt in my back pocket for my wad, peeled off ten twenties and dropped them on to the coffee table. 'There you go.' I saw he was about to object, and added, 'It's a loan. Pay me back when you can.'

'It might be a while.'

I shrugged my lack of concern and downed my coffee. 'No rush, Bill. We're mates. We go back a long way.' I looked pointedly at my watch. 'I've got to shoot off.'

He walked me to the door and patted my arm. 'Thanks for the loan. Don't leave it so long next time. And good luck.'

I gave him a puzzled frown and opened my mouth as if to speak.

'Why you came here,' he explained. 'The finger breaking job.'

'Oh, that,' I said. 'I think I might have over-reacted. I've changed my mind. I might let that one go.'

Bill smiled. 'Can't have been that important.'

'You're right. It wasn't. See you soon.'

★

Bob Hughes's first night at the Liquid Velvet created problems with some of the other doormen. Roger started mouthing off behind his back, telling me he'd been there much longer and why wasn't he put in charge in Jack's absence. I could have told him the truth, that his lack of tact and intelligence let his mouth off the lead too often. He didn't intend being rude or offhand to customers, but he had a bad attitude and lacked professionalism. Instead, I lied, and told him Bob had been in charge in loads of northern clubs and I had promised him the job some time ago. Tony didn't seem to care one way or the other, in fact, he was probably happier not having the responsibility of leadership. But Kevin, who was usually easy to manage, started behaving as if he'd been deeply insulted. His body language became bizarrely introspective, his shoulders hunched as if he had something to hide, and he stared at his feet, avoiding catching anyone's eye. It was uncharacteristic behaviour, but I didn't pay too much attention at the time, and put it down to him having another issue, like problems at home with his wife. But when my mobile rang early the following morning...

'Blimey, Kevin!' I said. I was still in my dressing gown, slurping my second coffee, glancing at Michelle's *Daily Mail* in the kitchen. 'It's not ten o'clock yet. What's up? Couldn't you sleep?'

'I wanted a word, Freddie. It might be important.'

'If it's about putting Bob in as a deputy for Jack, try not to eat your heart out. I explained my reasons to Roger.'

His next words were drowned by terrible rattling sounds, and then he shouted, 'Hang on, Freddie!' Eventually the background noise from wherever he was phoning became quieter, and he said, 'That's better.'

'Where you phoning from?' I asked.

'Main road near me. Thought I'd get a cooked breakfast at Wetherspoon's, but I wanted to ring you first. I can hear you better now, I've just turned off into a quieter road.'

I stifled my sudden impatience and asked him what the problem was.

'It's about this Bob Hughes bloke. Jack says he's OK but I ain't so sure.'

I stared at a photograph of the Chancellor of the Exchequer on the front page of the *Mail*, making him look even more insipid than usual, only half-listening to Kevin, who I suspected was making a fuss because of his resistance to change. I remembered it had taken him a long time to accept Jack as the man in charge, but after a few weeks Jack could do no wrong.

'You still there, Freddie?'

'Yes,' I replied. 'Spill it out. What's wrong with Bob Hughes then?'

'According to you and Jack, he lived up north, and done a short stretch in Walton.'

'Yeah, well, I like people to be up front about that sort of thing. I mean, I often bend the rules when I can, and some of you have been inside one time or another.'

'Exactly. I told you I did some time at Maidstone, didn't I?'

'Yeah, and I appreciate it was open and honest of you, Kev. But where is this leading?'

His voice became more excitable now. 'That's where I seen him before. Maidstone. He spent some time at Maidstone, waiting to be transferred to Parkhurst.'

I was suddenly alert now, and pressed the mobile closer to my ear. 'Isle of Wight… maximum security. You sure it's him?'

'Ninety-nine per cent. There can't be two people with that bottle scar.'

'No, that does seem pretty… conclusive,' I admitted. 'How long ago was this?'

''Bout eight years ago.'

'So if he's lying about where and how long he did a stretch, it must have been something serious. And you're sure it's the same bloke?'

'I'm certain it's him, Freddie.'

'What about the time at Maidstone? Did he recognise you, d'you think?'

'I don't know. I don't think so. Once I'd sussed out who he was, I tried to avoid looking at him.'

So that would explain Kevin's body language from the previous night.

'Listen, Kevin,' I said, 'thanks for letting me know, but I'd be much obliged if you'd keep this to yourself for the time being. You told anyone else?'

'I wanted to speak to you first.'

'Thanks. It's one I owe you, mate.'

'What you gonna do, Freddie?'

'First off I'll make a few enquiries and take it from there. Jack'll be back hopefully towards the middle of next week. If necessary I can always drop in most nights until then. Anyway, you have a good breakfast, Kev. And try not to drink too much.'

I heard him laughing.

'You kidding! I have coffee with my breakfast just so I can look down on all the Wetherspoon alkys. See you later, Freddie.'

I cut the call and sat staring into space for a moment, wondering what was going on with Bob Hughes. If that was his real name, which I seriously doubted after what Kevin had just told me. Now my gut instinct warned me to be on the lookout for something dark and dirty intruding on my turf. On the other hand, maybe I was worrying unduly. Perhaps Hughes, out of necessity, had been forced to lie and change his identity in order to get a job. But there was still a niggling suspicion growing in my mind like a fungal disease as I thought about his pally relationship with Jack, and how that had come about. I was determined to get to the bottom of what was going on and find out who this Bob Hughes really was.

I knew Jack wasn't called for his first night shoot until seven that evening, so I sent him a text asking him to meet ASAP. He replied within minutes, saying he was working out at the gym, and Hughes would be there later. I sent him another message, telling him the meeting was urgent and not to let Hughes know about it and we arranged to meet outside New Cross Gate underground station at 12:00 noon.

★

I found a parking space near the gym and walked round to the station. I was a little early and lit a cigarette from my packet of ten. I'd been trying to give up but had only managed to cut it down to ten a day. Michelle doesn't smoke and doesn't like the smell of it, either on my clothes or my breath. But I had managed to drop from thirty a day to sometimes less than ten. And I always carried a pack of Airwaves chewing gum to get rid of the tobacco breath for when I got home.

Bang on the dot of twelve, Jack suddenly materialised out of the crowd, carrying a sport holdall, sweat glistening on his forehead. His inscrutable expression belied the worry in his eyes.

'What's up?' he asked.

I got straight to the point. 'I have it on good authority that Bob Hughes is not who he says he is.'

'So who is he, Freddie?'

'That's just it: I haven't got a clue. But I intend to find out.'

Jack shook his head rapidly, as if he didn't believe me. 'Who told you this?'

'It doesn't matter, Jack. But I found out that Bob Hughes has done at least five years in Parkhurst. Which means he had a sentence of maybe seven or eight for a serious criminal offence. So how come you became pals at the gym? Who talked to who first?'

Jack frowned deeply as he thought about this, and I could see him forming questions in his mind.

'Now you come to mention it,' he said after a long pause, 'I think he spoke to me first; asked me where I worked and all that. Yeah, that's it. He wanted to know if there were any jobs going and then, when this filming job came up for me, he mentioned it again, asking if the Liquid Velvet would be short staffed and could he cover for me. What the hell's going on, Freddie?'

I shrugged. 'I wish I knew. He still at the gym now?'

Jack nodded.

'And what sort of car does he drive?'

'A black BMW, P reg. You going to follow him?'

'Yeah, I'd like to know where he lives, who he hangs out with, who his friends are. And, most of all, what his real name is.'

Jack looked genuinely upset, staring at me like a contrite schoolboy. 'I'm sorry, Freddie. I really am.'

'What about?'

'I feel responsible.'

I forced a smile and patted his arm. 'You weren't to know, Jack. Don't worry, I'll sort it.'

'At least you won't have long to wait. He said he's got to shoot off – he's leaving the gym at half-twelve.'

'Good,' I said. 'I'll find out what his game is.'

'Let me know, will you, Freddie? I'm filming tonight, but you can always send me a text.'

'I'll do that. I hope it goes well. Break a leg, as they say.'

'Yeah, thanks, Freddie. See you back at the Velvet the week after next.'

Jack sauntered off towards his flat, not far from New Cross Gate, and I hurried round to the gym, hoping Hughes didn't leave earlier than he said he was going to, in case I bumped into him. I had a quick look for his BMW and spotted it parked only about thirty metres from where I had parked my Jag, fortunately pointing in the same direction as mine. It was 12:10 and I wouldn't have long to wait. I got into the car, switched on Radio 2, and after two minutes of Jeremy Vine and a discussion about policing demonstrations, I switched it off and put my 'Queen Greatest Hits' CD on instead, and it had just played up to the fourth track, 'Fat Bottomed Girls,' when I saw Hughes coming out of the gym. I switched off the CD so I could concentrate on following his BMW and turned the ignition key.

He was definitely a boy racer, and his BMW roared past my Jag, the bass on his music player pounding out a chav beat. I pulled out and left a gap between us of a good fifty yards. He didn't know what sort of car I drove but, just to be on the safe side, as soon as we pulled out into the busy main road I let another car get between his and mine.

We headed round the one-way system towards Lewisham and after about two miles I saw his left indicator blinking. I slowed down as I didn't want to get too close now he was leaving the main road. As I turned left, I saw him racing towards the end of the street, past a block of flats where he turned right. I sped after him to the end of the street and I was just in time to see him pull up outside a small, scruffy pub. I braked sharply to avoid turning into the street in which the pub was situated and parked up. I could just about make out the name of the pub, The Alma. I sat and waited, hoping he wasn't about to indulge in a long boozy session. But after only a minute, he and another young bloke, arms completely smothered in tattoos, came dashing out of the pub, got into the BMW and drove off at great speed.

I thought about following them but decided against it. I felt I might learn more about Bob Hughes's real identity from the landlord or barman at the pub, especially if this was his manor and he was a regular there. I locked the Jag, crossed the road and entered The Alma.

As I pushed open the door, an elderly man and a woman, sitting at a corner table, nursing pints of stale looking bitter, gave me a cursory nod, both curious and suspicious, because I was an intruding stranger in their local. Behind the bar, a tall, thin man, with a craggy wrinkled face, a Ronnie Wood lookalike, glanced up from his copy of the *Sun*.

'Yes, guv, what can I get you?'

I scanned the top shelf. 'Gordon's and tonic with ice. And have a drink yourself.'

'Cheers, mate! I'll have a half with you.'

As soon as I'd been served, I leant across the bar and lowered my voice. 'That bloke who just left – bloke with the bottle scar – I'm sure I know him. Is his name Bob Hughes?'

The landlord filled his half pint glass with Guinness and casually looked me up and down. 'You with the Met, are you?'

I shook my head. 'Do I look like a copper?'

'As a matter of fact, you do. But no, you couldn't be the filth, else you'd know who that was. He's not long been out after a well-deserved rest courtesy of Her Majesty's government.'

'Parkhurst, weren't it?'

'So I believe. And you got the first name right. But it ain't Bob Hughes. It's Bob Crystal.'

It took a while for the name to register. When it did, I felt a tightening in my stomach.

'Something to do with the Crystal brothers?' I asked, frowning and guessing what the answer would be.

'His old man's doing two life sentences. He won't stroll along the leafy glades of South London again.'

'Dave Crystal still about, is he?'

Realising the couple in the corner had stopped speaking and were eavesdropping on our conversation, the landlord leant closer to me and spoke barely above a whisper.

'I take it you're referring to his wicked uncle. 'Bout time someone put him away an' all. The whole family's…' He swivelled a screw loose finger at the side of his head. 'That's why I don't like having Bob Crystal in here. Thank Christ he only come by to pick up his mate.'

'What was he sent down for?'

The landlord's mouth tightened. 'GBH. Victim almost died. I bet he wished he had by the time Crystal was through with him. The man's a psycho, seriously dangerous. Seems normal and calm on the surface, then bingo! Something goes click in his head and he turns into a monster.'

'Even so,' I said, 'an eight-year sentence seems steep for GBH.'

'Not when it's a hat trick. His first GBH was as a juvenile offender. He won't be happy until he kills someone.'

This was bad news indeed, and the tightening in my stomach started to feel distinctly loose now. I knocked back the G & T, thanked the landlord for the information, and left pretty sharpish.

5

THE PROPOSITION

Sean, manager of Liquid Velvet, usually arrives at the club early afternoon, so I drove to a car park I know close to Mile End Tube station, which was a great deal cheaper than the West End rate – plus avoiding the congestion charge – and caught the Central Line to Oxford Circus. As I walked down Kingley Street to the south side of Soho, I remembered Phil the Greek's club and made a mental note to give him a bell to see if he'd considered using my services.

When I got to the Velvet I found Sean ensconced in his office, fiddling about on his computer on his clutter-free desk. I think he loves his office, which looks more like a private room in a St James's gentleman's club with its gilt-framed equestrian oil paintings and expensive furnishings.

I knocked and entered the office hurriedly and he looked up in surprise. He hadn't expected to see me at this time of day and his forehead creased into a worried frown as he caught my anxious expression. His face, redder than usual, exposed his hedonistic lifestyle in its handsome but slightly bloated appearance, but his blue eyes were clear and bright under a mop of blonde hair. He even spoke in the posh vowels of Mayor Boris, although I have always suspected Sean of coming from a humble background.

'Sean,' I began as I occupied one of his comfortable leather chairs, 'Sorry to disturb you but we have a problem.'

'We?' he queried, making it sound as if my problem was mine alone and he had no intention of getting involved.

'What do you know about a Dave Crystal?'

He sat back and regarded me through shrewd, narrowed eyes. 'Villain from south of the river. Dangerous, nasty, vicious – an egomaniac…' He suddenly flashed me a wide grin and gestured palms up. 'Allegedly!'

'Have you ever had any dealings with him, Sean?'

'We crossed swords not long ago.'

I felt one of those sudden lurches, throwing me off balance. 'What!?' I exclaimed.

'Yes, unfortunately he graced us with his presence at the Velvet. He and his cohorts behaved in an unbecoming manner and were asked to leave.'

'And they left without assistance?'

'Yes, but not without making all kinds of threats. Their language was appalling. I barred him, of course. And that was the night Lady Antonia Disscorn was here. Mind you, *her* language between the sheets is something to be marvelled at.'

He smiled at the memory, but I was in no mood for frivolity.

'So Dave Crystal threatened to get back at you for barring him. How come I didn't know about this?'

'You were on holiday in Cuba, dear boy, trying to improve on your fake tan. And, after Mr Crystal had given us his dire warnings, we were all on guard for weeks afterwards, but nothing happened. I assumed it was all so much hot air.'

'It could be a costly assumption, Sean.'

Sean glanced at his Rolex and sighed. 'I don't want to be rude, dear boy, but could we er…'

'Cut to the chase?' I said. 'Sure. Jack recommended this new bouncer, Bob Hughes. But it seems as if he was set up. Bob Hughes is none other than Bob Crystal, Dave Crystal's nephew.'

'Curiouser and curiouser.'

Sean appeared not to be taking my predicament very seriously. I injected some agitation into my tone. 'Bob Crystal has spent most of his life behind bars. Even as a juvenile offender he did time for grievous bodily harm. He has a nasty habit of half-killing people. Literally.'

'I see,' Sean said after a thoughtful pause. 'So Dave Crystal gives his nephew a cock and bull story about getting a job here in the hopes that he'll freak out one night and injure one of our customers.'

'You're not just a pretty face, Sean.'

'So what are you going to do, dear boy?'

I felt a dryness in my throat as I spoke. 'I don't have many options.'

'Well one thing's for certain now that you've told me about Bob Crystal, I'm going to have to kick him into touch.' He threw me an apologetic, sympathetic look, but it wasn't overly sincere and even added, a touch unnecessarily, I thought, 'I'd hate to be in your shoes when you make that phone call.'

'Yeah, thanks, Sean' I said as I rose and headed for the door. 'Don't bother sending flowers. Just open a bottle of Bollinger and toast me with crocodile tears.'

'Oh, Freddie,' he said, and I stopped halfway out of the door, thinking he was going to add something helpful. How wrong could I be?

'As Bob Hughes né Crystal won't be doing the shift tonight, may I ask who will be?'

Irritated, I snapped, 'I'll be back later.'

'You're a Godsend!' He waved a dismissive hand at me and turned his attention back to the computer.

★

After I'd been home and given Michelle the bad news that I had to work that night, I went out into the garden and made the call on my mobile.

'Bob,' I said, 'Freddie Weston here.'

I could hear music blaring in the background with Bob Crystal shouting over it, 'Hang on, Freddie.' Then it went quiet. 'That's better. What can I do for you, mate?'

'Look something's cropped up and I'd like to talk to you about a little proposition. Can you meet me in Soho at five?'

'Whereabouts?'

'What about the Coach and Horses in Greek Street?'

'I don't know it.'

'Just off Shaftsbury Avenue, back of the Palace Theatre. Ask someone if you can't find it. It's a very well-known watering hole.

And bring an overnight bag with you. I want you to go north for the night and come back tomorrow.'

'What's it all about?'

'I'll tell you later, Bob. See you then.'

I ended the call, wondering if I was making the right decision. But first I needed to do a couple of internet searches, so I went back inside the house, hoping Michelle had left by now to give Olivia a lift home from school.

★

The Coach and Horses was fairly busy when I got there, but I still managed to find one quiet corner where I might have a word with Bob without fear of being overheard. The few necessary items he would need for the job were in the Sainsbury's orange carrier bag I was carrying, and I placed it on the floor by the leg of my chair.

When he arrived, only a few minutes after me, I offered to buy him a drink and he asked for a pint of Kronenbourg.

'Cheers, Freddie!' he said after I'd got his beer. 'What's on your mind?'

No sense in beating about the bush, so I got straight to the point. 'How would you like to earn in one night what it would take you three weeks to earn in the club?'

He stared at me with cold, impassive eyes and there was a hint of suspicion in his tone. 'What would I have to do?'

I glanced over my shoulder before I told him quietly, 'Take a trip to Manchester and break someone's fingers for me. I'll pay you a grand plus expenses. I'd like you to go up there tonight.'

'What about the club?'

'Don't worry about that. It'll be sorted till Jack gets back. Then I'll see if I can find you something else.'

He was silent for a while and his stare was unnerving in its coldness. 'You mean you don't need me at the Velvet no more?'

'We've got all the staff we need. But by tomorrow morning you should be back on the train heading south a grand richer. How bad is that?'

'Who's the target?'

'Lead guitarist of a group called Electroganic.'

Crystal's eyes lit up and he suddenly became animated. 'No! Not Electroganic!'

'Shh!' I hissed. 'Keep your voice down.'

He chuckled and lowered his voice, which was strained with incredulity. 'I can't believe you're asking me to break Kyle Henson's fingers.'

'You know this group then.'

'I've got an album of theirs. They're a fucking good group. Jesus Christ! What's the geezer done to you?'

The question I'd been dreading. If I avoided telling him the truth – or part of the truth – he might think this was some record industry scam involving loads of money and he would want a bigger fee.

'He was fucking around with my daughter,' I said after a moment's hesitation. 'Treated her badly.'

He wasn't interested in details. He was too taken with the celebrity of the group, and chuckled delightedly again. 'I can't believe you're asking me to break Kyle Henson's fingers.'

'As long as you get well paid, what do you care?'

He stopped laughing and nodded seriously. 'Yeah. Right.'

'And if you're happy with the arrangement,' I continued, 'will you let your uncle Dave know you're sorted work-wise?'

I watched this sink in, but his face showed little emotion.

'How did you find out?'

'Just by chance, someone recognised you. It doesn't matter who.'

'Uncle Dave knew I wouldn't stand much chance getting a job as doorman, not with my form.'

'So he had the idea of a change of identity and getting you in with Jack. Why did he do that, d'you suppose?'

'He was looking after my interests.'

'That was very considerate of him.'

If he noticed the sarcasm in my voice, his face didn't register it.

'But as long as he knows you're happy with our little arrangement,' I went on, 'then he won't have any grumbles, will he?'

'True. But just one thing, I expect you want this Kyle creep to suffer.'

'Finger a time's what I had in mind.'

He sucked in his breath noisily and shook his head. 'Bastard'll scream blue murder. Could be dodgy getting away. I mean, we are dealing with a celebrity here. Not just any old loser.'

I knew what he was getting at and said, 'I think a grand for finger breaking's already way over the odds.'

'I think it's gotta be worth at least fifteen-hundred. It's a tricky one. He's so fucking well known, be hard to get him on his own.'

'I'm sure you'll manage it,' I smiled. 'OK, fifteen-hundred it is. Deal.'

We shook hands on it and I handed him an envelope. 'I'd thought of half as down payment, paying the balance on a result. There's seven-hundred in there, the other two hundred being expenses. I'll give you the other grand as soon as you get back – job done, of course.'

The envelope disappeared inside his brown leather jacket and a pervy glint came into his eye. 'So what did this wanker actually do to your daughter?'

I gave him a hard look. 'Don't go there. You don't need to know. All right?'

'Sorry, Freddie, just curious, that's all.'

'Oh, and another thing, don't get carried away.'

'What's that supposed to mean?'

'It means just his fingers, no other rough treatment.'

'What do you care, Freddie?'

'I care if the bloke dies, Bob. He's a guitarist, and the broken fingers might end his slimy career... for a while at least. That's going to be justice enough.'

Bob patted my arm and smiled. 'Don't worry, Freddie, mate. Fingers only. Trust me.'

Like I trusted a pit bull with a toddler. But I could think of no other way out of my predicament. I was being swept along now with my crazy scheme, hanging on to the futile hope that Dave Crystal would let me off the hook and find some other way to get back at the club.

Yeah, chance would be a fine thing! But I hoped my generosity towards his vile nephew might at least buy me some time.

I took a slip of paper out of my shirt pocket and handed it to young Crystal. 'Details are on there,' I told him. 'Electroganic are playing at Manchester Arena, staying at the Radisson Edwardian Hotel and I've booked you in under the name of Hugh Roberts. I got the name and address out the phone book. Once the police are called they're bound to check on occupants who stayed a single night. The poor sod whose name I took will have a visit from the law, but they'll soon find out it was random. You need to pay eighty cash when you check in, using the name and address I've given you, and then you can clear out after the job's done.'

Crystal nodded, thoughtfully chewing his lip. 'You've thought of everything.'

'Yeah, and I've even thought of what you're going to tell your uncle Dave, because there's no way anyone else can know about this. Show him the colour of the money and tell him I'm paying you for some bodyguard work, protecting me for the next month. Remember, it's vital only us two know about this. Otherwise…' I paused and gave him a long hard look. 'You know what could happen.'

'Yeah. Next time they'll throw away the key.'

I picked up the Sainsbury's carrier bag. 'Stick that in your holdall.'

'What is it?'

'Some rope and a roll of gaffer tape. You'll need to silence those screams as much as possible, but make sure you let him breathe. And you'll need to tie him up afterwards. If you stick the "Do Not Disturb" sign on the door no one'll find him until late the next morning, which'll give you a chance to leave at a reasonable hour. It might look odd if you were to vacate your room at some ungodly hour. This way you'll go unnoticed with all the other guests coming down to breakfast and checking out.'

There was a look of admiration in his eyes as he said, 'Fuck me! You really have thought this through, haven't you?'

I shrugged and gave him a half smile. 'Well, we've got to make sure it goes smoothly, for both our sakes.'

Not wanting to spend another minute in his company, I wished him luck, told him to relax and finish his drink, and took my leave of him. As I walked along Shaftsbury Avenue, I felt slightly nauseous. Either it was the dust and diesel fumes or it was a feeling of disgust mixed with guilt at the pain I had conspired to inflict on another human being.

But I was committed now. Of course, I could have called Crystal on his mobile and called him off, let him keep the money I'd given him as a down payment. But I'm a family man. And family and friends are the fundamental reason for my existence. Anyone does the dirty on them will suffer the consequences. And you don't have to be an amateur psychiatrist to see how this attitude developed. From the day my father went upstairs and hanged himself because he was being blackmailed by that bastard Lennox, I swore revenge on anyone who harmed my loved ones. And I have always felt frustrated that I could never find the slightest bit of proof against Lennox. Maybe I never would. But it didn't take much analysis to work out that the guitarist was a substitute.

Too bad. He had treated Jackie like shit, so now he was going to have to pay the price, up in that hotel room in Manchester, in the small inebriated hours of the morning. I could picture the scene.

★

Kyle Henson slept fitfully, the alcohol in his bloodstream penetrating his nervous system and brain, obstructing a deeper oblivion. Had he been asleep for hours or minutes? He had no way of knowing.

He could have sworn he heard a knock. A light tap on the door. Or was it on an adjoining wall. And there it was again. Definitely a knock on the door. He blinked sleep from his eyes and tried to clear his head as he swung his legs out of the bed. Maybe it was one of the others in the band. Kevin, the drummer, was the one who always wanted to continue well into wee small hours. As he staggered towards the door, he caught sight of the bedside clock. It was just gone five-thirty.

'Who is it?' he croaked, his voice hoarse from too much booze, tobacco and dope.

'Room service, sir. Complimentary champagne.'

At 5:30 in the morning? He knew they'd all had a late night, but what the fuck! He carefully pressed the door handle down and started to peer out, his vision blurred. Which was when the door hit him in the chest, but the pain didn't register at first. A hand shoved him backwards as the door slammed shut, and he fell back, crashing into the built-in dressing table. His legs buckled and he collapsed on the floor. A man who looked like your typical thug stood over him, his face a blur of aggression and cruelty.

'Hello, Kyle,' the thug said, greeting him like he was an old mate.

'Shit, man!' Kyle managed to say. 'What's going on?'

'Shame!' said the thug. 'I thought Electroganic was a good group.'

'Was? What are you talking about? We still are?'

He felt helpless as the thug stood over him, smiling now and taking something out of the pocket of his grey leather jacket.

Kyle tried to crawl away, opening his mouth to cry out for help. Which was when the fist hit him in the side of his head, slamming him into the carpet. And then, as he lay semi-conscious, a sickening smell of plastic as something tasting of acetate was wound around his mouth. He started to scream but it came out as a moan, muffled by the gag.

Nothing happened for a moment. He thought he heard a click. Followed by loud voices, unreal, a man's voice booming about the economy. It was the television, the sound distorted and reverberating.

And then he was pulled roughly onto his back, and the thug pressed a foot into his right armpit and raised his arm, twisting it at an angle away from his body. He felt the vicious fingers enclosing his own, feeling for leverage for the first index finger. That was when the torture began and he heard his own screams, alarming and frightening in their intensity. And there was even more unbearable pain being inflicted on him, like the worst toothache he had ever experienced, as each finger was snapped systematically. By the time the thug had reached the little finger, the torture was over because he had passed out.

6
ROID RAGE

At seven in the evening the shit hit the fan. Michelle came storming into the kitchen, having caught the six o'clock news at a friend's house. Luckily both our daughters were out, because I could see by the flushed look on her face and the desperation in her eyes and the way her hands trembled uncontrollably like someone with Parkinson's as she struggled to formulate her thoughts and assemble them into coherent speech, that she was as uptight as I've ever seen her. Worry lines were like scars on her forehead and she looked as if she was fighting to stem the flow of tears.

Not that I could blame her. I hadn't anticipated this guitarist – mainly because I'd never heard of him and his poxy group – becoming the major item on the news.

'I hope you've seen the news,' Michelle shouted, looking over her shoulder in case one of our girls was present, although she knew they were both out. 'I hope that wasn't anything to do with you, Freddie. Please tell me it wasn't you.'

I shrugged innocently. 'What are you talking about, Michelle? The enquiry into the phone hacking scandal or…'

I didn't get a chance to finish. Her eyes blazed as her voice became piercingly loud. 'I mean that fucking guitarist. You know damn well what I'm talking about.'

'Calm down, my dear,' I told her, before I realised now was not the best time to do a Michael Winner impression.

Crash! My wine glass – which I had fortunately drained when I heard her arriving home – hit the bottom of a cupboard and smashed into tiny fragments.

'Christ!' I exclaimed. 'Steady on, Michelle. There's no need to smash the place up. We can talk about this.'

'That's what I'm trying to do. But you… you…'

She sank heavily into a chair by the kitchen table, her shoulders slumped and I could see she was close to tears. I went and placed a hand on her shoulder but she shrugged it away.

'Don't lie to me, Freddie. That guitarist who had his fingers broken. That was you, wasn't it?'

I turned my back on her, going to the cupboard under the sink to fetch a dustpan and brush to clear up the broken glass. 'I was at the Liquid Velvet most of the night. Seen by hundreds of people. If that's not a perfect alibi, I don't know what is.'

'I don't mean you personally. No doubt you got one of your dodgy friends to do it. And when the police start to investigate what happened, they might – just might – be able to point the finger at you. Then what? You could go to jail for years if they catch you.'

'That's not going to happen,' I said, stooping to sweep up the glass, which seemed to have gone everywhere.

'No? How can you be so sure?'

'I just know, that's all.'

Perhaps it was because of my confidence and my relaxed demeanour, or the way I was focused on my task of clearing up the mess, but Michelle suddenly drifted into a thoughtful silence and I could almost hear the wheels spinning in her head, whirring with combinations of questions and concerns. I tipped the glass from the pan into the pedal bin and waited for her next condemnation of the guitarist stunt. When she eventually spoke, there was a quiet tremor and a rasp in her voice.

'And what about Jackie, when she finds out?'

I sat facing Michelle at the other end of the table and told her, 'Jackie's bound to find out. After all, she was a fan of the group. And even if she doesn't see it on the news, she's bound to hear about it from one of her mates. But she's not going to know why he had his fingers broken, is she? She doesn't know what we know about her and the…' I swallowed noisily and chased the intruding image from my mind. 'She won't think there's any connection whatsoever.'

The way Michelle looked at me, I could see I was losing her respect. She regarded me like some sort of wacko she didn't understand or know, or even want to know. I realised I had stupidly damaged our relationship and it would take some time to heal. She wouldn't trust me for a while, and I knew that at the back of her mind was the desperate suspicion that if I ever found out what Lennox had done to my old man, I'd be hell-bent on revenge.

Yes, her look spoke volumes. I was now the working-class oik, tarnished with a shady background, an East End upbringing she saw as an almost comic book picture of villains wielding razors and baseball bats as they threatened poor shopkeepers for protection money. Whereas she'd been raised in the wilds of middle-class Surrey by Mr and Mrs Don and Rita Brown. A suburb of Esher, which to me is a suburb in itself. Michelle's parents' home was near a parade of shops, not far from a busy roundabout, near which stood a large mock-Tudor pub. The district was dull and lifeless and, after we were married, every time we went to visit their parents in their – again, mock-Tudor – semi, I experienced a sinking feeling, not unlike the sensation of drowning in something deep and glutinous. Maybe it was just me, the big city boy, but I couldn't stand the area. I was grateful when our children were growing up, making our visits more bearable, seeing as how they would entertain her parents and help the stultifying time pass reasonably quickly until it was time to escape back to London. I have to admit, although I was full of sympathy for Michelle and her mother, when Mr Brown suffered a coronary and died six years ago, I was relieved we would never have to set eyes on Esher again, because Michelle persuaded her mother to move to sheltered accommodation only a twenty minute drive from our place, and she is now able to call on her regularly but for shorter visits. I accompany Michelle on sporadic visits from a sense of duty and because her mother seems always to have accepted how I provide for my family without question, even though I don't think she fully understands what it is I really do. Whereas I always felt Michelle's father regarded me warily, with feelings of distrust. Even my love of cooking cast me as some sort of alien freak, in spite of there being enough male chefs dominating our airwaves. But then Don Brown had never so much as boiled an egg in his life. Every evening, after returning home from work where he owned and managed an old-fashioned gentleman's outfitters, he would find his dinner on the table. The semi was kept spotless and Don invariably took refuge from Rita's obsessive vacuuming and dusting with obsessive gardening, pruning and planting at all hours. But I always felt, especially by the owl-like way he stared at me when I answered one of his probing questions, that his mind was shoving me into one of his preconceived compartments, where I would be labelled as a dodgy character in his secret cabinet file. And I don't think it was paranoia on my part, because even Michelle had noticed it and stood up for me on several occasions. But now I could see her delving into her father's filing cabinet, and taking out the folder which denounced me as a shady character, while good old Don muttered 'I told you so' from beyond the grave.

I braced myself for the next instalment.

'Why?' she sniffed, after a sullen silence. 'Why did you do it, Freddie?'

'To teach the bloke a lesson.'

She laughed bitterly. 'Oh, yes? And how is he going to learn that lesson, seeing as how you wouldn't have told him why you had that done to him? At least, I hope you weren't stupid enough to do that.'

'Of course not,' I mumbled.

'Well then? What was the point of it?'

'I was hoping he might guess the reason someone had it in for him. *And* it was a way of getting closure for what he did to our daughter.'

'Oh, don't give me that bollocks, Freddie.'

I sighed pointedly, letting my breath out like a deflating balloon. 'If it's any consolation, Michelle, I deeply regret it now. I really do.'

Her mouth twitched into a sarcastic smirk.

'No, really. The things is, I have a problem with one of my bouncers and I thought giving him the job of breaking the guitarist's fingers would help me out of a tight spot.'

'That doesn't make any sense.'

I cleared my throat, knowing I was going to have to tell her about Bob Crystal and his uncle. First I got up, fetched two wine glasses and white wine from the fridge, but when I started to pour her a glass, she indicated for me to stop when it was half full and said, 'I've got to pick Olivia up from her friend's at seven.' I sat down again, and launched into my tale of woe, telling her about my mistake of employing Bob Crystal and the way his uncle wanted to avenge himself on the Liquid Velvet. At the end of my story, she nodded thoughtfully, and I could see I might have gained a little sympathy and understanding of why I'd behaved like a shifty sadist, employing someone else to do what an angry father should have done himself, if he was that way inclined. Which, I have to admit, I was.

'And you think this will keep his uncle happy?' Michelle said, incredulity in her tone. 'He's still going to want to get his revenge on the club, and you taking the doorman's job away from his nephew will still piss him right off.'

'Yeah, big time,' I agreed. 'But I told Bob Crystal to tell his uncle he'd be getting well over doormen's wages just to do some personal bodyguard work for me. And I've heard rumours that Mark Lennox is making a bid for the Kismet Club. So if I put Bob Crystal on the door at the Kismet and Lennox takes over, he won't want to employ my staff, that's for sure.'

I saw Michelle shiver and her eyes clouded over.

'What's wrong? You're not cold, are you?'

'I was thinking of this Crystal bloke.'

'Which one? The uncle or the nephew?'

'Nephew. What if he goes berserk and beats someone up like he did before?'

I took a sip of wine before answering. It was something I'd considered, and it was also something I didn't want on my conscience.

'I'm hoping,' I said, 'Lennox will take over the Kismet very soon, and Jack will be back at the Velvet. Lennox knows I won't have anything to do with supplying him with doormen, so he'll probably get rid of Bob Crystal and employ his own staff.'

'Well, let's just hope for your sake – all our sakes – that this Crystal thug doesn't kill someone before then.'

I stared into my wine glass and could feel Michelle peering across the table's expanse at the worried frown on my face.

'Why d'you suppose he freaks out like that?' she said. 'From what you've told me, one minute he's quiet and reasonably intelligent, then something snaps in his head and turns him into a savage bastard.'

'Have you heard of roid rage?'

'Vaguely, but I don't know much about it.'

'I looked it up online. I think Bob Crystal's into body building and takes anabolic steroids. All that extra testosterone can have negative effects and result in extreme male aggression like a light being switched on. Behaviour changes, swings into moods of depression and even schizophrenia.'

Michelle's voice dropped to an awesome whisper. 'Jesus, Freddie! You can't have him as one of your club bouncers for a single day. This is serious. What if he kills someone? Get rid of him immediately.'

'That's easier said than done. What about Dave Crystal?'

Michelle thumped the table with her fist. 'Why should this become your problem? I mean, we were on holiday when he and his thugs were asked to leave the Liquid Velvet. I don't think the manager of the club's being very supportive. It should be his problem, seeing as you were thousands of miles away when it happened.'

'Yes, but I'm the one who's been set up via Jack. If I hadn't listened to Jack's recommendation, none of this would have happened. And if I hadn't followed Bob Crystal to that pub, I would never have known about the reasons for his jail sentence. It's become my headache, Michelle, and I'm the one who's going to have to sort it.'

'But giving this Bob Crystal a job at the Kismet's hardly going to solve your problems, is it? His uncle wants him at the Liquid Velvet so he can get his revenge.' Her eyes were as cold as glass as she stared at me. 'And you're just as bad as all those crooks and vicious bastards, with your plans for revenge. Isn't that what's wrong with the world? Everyone getting their own back on someone else. It's time to draw a line and say no more, Freddie. No more. But you always have to cross that line, don't you?'

Fortunately, after this diatribe, her eye came in contact with the kitchen clock and she rose hurriedly.

'Shit! It's 6:50. I've got to pick Olivia up and I'm going to be fifteen minutes late. We'll talk about this later.'

'Sorry, Michelle, Friday's our busy night. You know that. I have to go to the Velvet tonight. I haven't got Jack and I can't put Bob Crystal in there. And thinking of what you said about the club not being supportive, I might get there earlier and have a word with Sean – see what we can sort out.'

Michelle picked up her car keys off the table and dashed out, calling over her shoulder, 'Get him to apologise to this bloke's uncle and invite him back to the club.'

The front door slammed and I smiled grimly at her suggestion, which was about as likely to happen as Afghanistan entering a team of women for beach volleyball at the Olympics.

I topped up my wine and then switched on Channel 4 News to see if there were any more details about the assault in the Manchester hotel. The news was pretty much the same as the BBC's, with one exception: questions were asked about the guitarist's behaviour when it came to indulging his craving for young girl groupies, and his bad reputation caused much speculation in this area. And, although the reporter dropped hints that it could have been an angry parent, apparently Kyle Henson, who had already been interviewed by the police, was reluctant to offer any theory as to who might have broken his fingers or give any reason why anyone would want to do that. I knew the police would follow up the name Bob Crystal's hotel room was booked in and draw a blank, so I didn't think they would ever come knocking on my door over this incident. Job done. But I was far from proud of my actions, knowing I had shown myself to be as corrupt as some of the dodgy characters I had grown up with – villains who still inhabited my nightly haunts.

7
SKIVING OFF

When I arrived at the Liquid Velvet, I had a brief meeting with Sean and vainly attempted to press on him what Michelle had argued, that it had been his fault for banning Dave Crystal and I was collateral damage. But he merely shrugged it off, saying he was quite in order to ban who he liked, and turned the tables by telling me it was my responsibility to provide staff, and Jack and I had made the hiccup over Bob Crystal. Some hiccup, I explained to Sean, seeing as I was likely to get a severe beating – and that would be getting off lightly – by a couple of Dave Crystal's mob who would accuse me of fucking their boss's nephew about. But Sean was in no mood to listen to my miseries and curtailed the meeting by saying he had to meet a potential client who wanted to book the club for a Monday night. Liquid Velvet, one of the West End's most popular and prestigious clubs, is busy almost every night, but they have a policy of keeping Mondays closed to the general public so that it can either be hired for private functions or shut for one night.

'Private function doesn't come cheap,' I said as I was leaving his office. 'Anyone we might know?'

He told me it was another celebrity famous for appearing in magazines like *Hello!* and little else, and she was launching her autobiography, a kiss-and-tell tome about her on-off, on again then off again, relationship with an *X Factor* runner-up who had a number six in the charts with yet another version of 'I Write the Songs.'

'Another ghost-written autobiography,' I said. 'I can't wait.'

Sean grinned. 'What else d'you expect from a bimbo with big tits and a tan the colour of my piss on a bad morning?'

In spite of my gloom, I chuckled. 'You're very cynical, Sean. But I still don't think you'd kick her out of bed given a chance.'

He faked an exaggerated expression of horror. 'Dear boy, how wrong can you be? I do have certain standards, you know.'

After our little parting exchange, I walked to the foyer and took up a position by the entrance. My mood soured again as I thought about Dave Crystal, wondering how long it would be before he started intimidating me. I was under no illusions about the way it would go. First would come the threats and then, if I didn't reinstate his nephew, I'd be looking over my shoulder every night, waiting for the sudden violence. But the worst of an attack is the kicking a man gets when he's down. Broken ribs, missing teeth, and worst of all pissing blood because of damaged kidneys.

It wasn't something I wanted to risk at my age. I thought maybe I could call on a few favours from some of the villains I knew. The trouble was, most of the guys who once had an awesome reputation now like to think of themselves as businessmen – that's when they're not having their memoirs ghosted. And, although they've always been tribal over their selected territories, I knew they'd be reluctant to revert to the bad old days of gang warfare over what might be considered a petty dispute. Especially as most of them were well past their prime.

No, I had to think long and hard to find a way out of this predicament. And the only way to think long and hard is with a glass of something to assist the pondering. So I waited until Sean had left the building, then put Roger in charge of the main entrance, knowing he would make an effort to run things smoothly, hoping I would consider him as the main man should Jack start doing more work, which seemed likely as he seemed to be building a good reputation for himself.

As I walked across Golden Square towards Kingley Street, I took off my bow tie and stuck it in my pocket. I often wear an ordinary black lounge suit, so whenever I remove the bow I can skive off. Not that I'm unduly worried about shirking, because strictly speaking

I haven't been a doorman for years. But when you run your own company, you have to go back to the coal face occasionally.

I intended to see if Phil the Greek at the Jax had made up his mind about my company providing him with doormen. Unfortunately, he wasn't on the premises and the second in command couldn't help me. So I had a drink in the less busy upstairs bar, which was still subjected to the pounding from the cellar and dance floor below. After I'd found a small alcove seat, a steady throb like a ship's engine reverberated under my feet. I swigged from a bottle of over-priced premium lager, and wondered why the manager of the establishment hadn't put in an appearance on a Friday night, but in the back of my mind there were far more niggling concerns, and I brooded about the Crystal problem. I didn't think he knew why his uncle wanted him working at the Velvet. In fact, I was convinced he wouldn't have minded which club he fronted as a doorman, as long as he had a job, and was able to use his daylight hours to train and pump iron. And Dave Crystal must have known about the roid rage — maybe it had been used in his nephew's defence at his trial. So the evil bastard didn't care if someone got seriously injured or killed and his nephew was put away for life. And all for what? Just because he was barred from a club. Talk about an over-reaction. But then that's what it's like when you cross some of those demented thugs. I remembered the story about Ronnie Kray shooting George Cornell in The Blind Beggar pub because the gangster called him a 'fat poof.' There may have been other reasons, but those are the sort of nutters who only need a thin excuse to murder someone.

I thought my best bet was to give Bob Crystal a job at the Kismet, knowing it wouldn't last, and hope the time he spent there before Lennox took over would pass without any major incidents.

But I was clutching at straws and still hadn't a clue how I was going to keep Dave Crystal from coming after me. As I swigged the last of my beer, over the bottom rim of the bottle a face swam into focus and my eyes met another pair which seemed to be studying me closely. I put the bottle down on the bamboo table and smiled at her.

She was striking — mid-thirties I guessed — with short dark hair and green eyes. She was no beauty, but her features were pronounced and not unattractive, almost as if she had been chiselled out of stone, and the make-up she wore was subtle and expertly applied. She certainly had bags of sex appeal and her expensive, pale grey suit was expertly fashioned and was close-fitting enough to show off her gorgeous figure. Just for a moment I wondered if she might be on the game, because she returned my smile and said, 'You were miles away.'

I put it to the test, to see if she was touting for business. I said, 'All on your own? Or were you hoping to meet someone?'

The smile changed to a little-girl pout. 'I was here on a date, and he stood me up.' She looked at her watch. 'We were supposed to meet here at eight, and it's now getting on for nine, so I guess that's it. I'm not a professional, if that's what you're thinking.'

I placed a hand over my heart. 'As if I would think such a thing.'

She chuckled, a throaty purr, her desirability bursting forth now.

Now that's the trouble with temptation – it's no fun unless you give in to it. And before I'd even thought about it, I had bought her and me another drink and she was sitting opposite me. I introduced myself. Real name, of course. No point in lying, seeing as I didn't plan on this going any further than a flirtation. And even if it did, I planned on laying out the ground rules, like how I was a happily married, family man, and a fling would be dangerous, but not out of the question provided discretion could be guaranteed.

But first things first. I needed to get to know this lady, whose name was Alison. I toasted her with my glass and said, 'So what work *do* you do, Alison?'

'Please call me Ali. All my friends do.'

'So what do you do, Ali?'

'I work for a cosmetics firm. In marketing.'

'As in bing-bong, Avon calling!'

She giggled and said, 'Cheeky sod! I'm not a door-to-door salesperson. I'm the manager of our marketing department. Office-based. And what do you do, Freddie?'

'I have my own business supplying doormen to many West End clubs – some in East London, too.'

Her eyes widened with sudden interest. 'You mean bouncers?'

I chuckled, feeling a warm glow from the drink. 'Yeah. Bouncers, if you like.'

'So I suppose you spend loads of time visiting all the nightspots? Must be quite an eye-opener.'

'How d'you mean?'

'Well, I've always imagined clubs attract all sorts of rogues and villains.'

'A fair few.'

'You must have quite a lot of stories to tell.'

'Enough to write a book, I should think. I know dozens of London gangsters. Grew up with most of them.'

'Wow! What an exciting life you must lead.'

I shrugged, demonstrating a reluctance to admit rubbing shoulders with the elite of London's underworld, but at the same time I realised she might get a kick from hearing yarns about gangsters. So I added with a teasing smile, 'You wouldn't believe some of the things I hear about.'

'Like what, for instance?'

'Like the geezer who committed a bank job in Brighton, and thought he'd take his wife and kiddies down and make a day of it. He couldn't find anywhere to park and having deposited the family on the pier, he was late for the robbery – they had started without him. But he joined in and they managed to get away with a half decent haul.'

She leant forwards, and her eyes lit up. 'Did they get caught?'

'Eventually. He got a ten stretch for that.'

'How long ago was this?'

'Back in the seventies.'

Deflated, she sat back and blew out her breath. 'Oh, that long ago. Not exactly hot off the press that story.'

I shrugged, peeved that she wasn't impressed by my first tale of villainy. 'I could tell you of more recent deeds,' I offered, hoping to draw her back in, 'but I have to be a bit careful. Otherwise…' I sliced my fingers across my throat.

She giggled. 'Well, I wouldn't want to get you into trouble. Not that I could pass on any information that would compromise you.'

I leant forwards, threw a cloak-and-dagger look over my shoulder, and dropped my voice to a conspiratorial level, although I had to compete with the basement music. 'Only last week, bloke who came in one of my clubs regularly – the Liquid Velvet – got sent down for fraud. And this bloke rubs shoulders with royalty and Russian oligarchs. Which means he'll get sent to a cushy open prison and he'll probably be allowed to cycle out for a cream tea on sunny afternoons.'

'He must be influential.'

'Oh, he is.'

'Would I have heard of him.'

'The Right Honourable Garston Welch.'

'The MP who falsely claimed expenses? I thought you were telling me about a gangster or a villain.'

I sat back and gave her a wide, knowing smile. 'Same difference. Just because he went to Eton and Oxford doesn't mean he's behaved any differently from any of the East End villains I know.'

'But that's already common knowledge. The papers were full of it. Come on, you must have some nice juicy stories from under the counter.

'Such as?'

She flashed me a highly flirtatious, eye-sparkling smile. 'Oh, you know, villains who have quite literally got away with murder.'

'Why are you so interested?' I asked after a pause.

'Oh, I've no great interest. I just thought it might be exciting to hear some awesome stories about gangsters, the ones the general public don't get to hear about.'

I laughed and shook my head. Whenever club punters get a hint of my background and my shady connections, more often than not they will pester me to satisfy their lust for a gossipy glimpse into the underworld, hoping some of the dirt will rub off on them, but from a safe distance. And I've often found that many women actually get off on associating with criminals, as long as they don't get too close to the action. So, in this respect, I fitted the bill perfectly. And on this occasion I decided I would exaggerate my bad boy image and have a bit of fun.

'I have to get back to the Liquid Velvet,' I said, glancing at my watch, 'but if you're interested in hearing some shocking stories – some of the unpublished ones – we could meet up for a bite to eat during next week.'

'I'd like that very much.'

I took out my mobile phone, she gave me her number and I keyed it in to my phone's address book. That done, I stood up, leant over and pecked her on each cheek. 'Good to meet you, Ali.'

'You too, Freddie.'

I turned and was about to walk away, when I thought I had better lay it on the line. 'By the way. I'm happily married and I have two teenage children.'

She smiled knowingly and tapped the side of her nose with an index finger. 'Don't worry, my middle name is discretion.'

It was music to my ears.

8

INCIDENT AT WALTHAMSTOW

Saturday night at the Liquid Velvet and I'd had enough of clubs. I wanted to get home and forget about night life, put it all behind me, settle down and get a proper job. I was going through one of those regular phases of not wanting to be involved with grimy nightlife and lowlife, but that's just what it was – a phase – and it would last about as long as it took me to escape from home after a quiet Sunday and a dreary Monday, when I would be itching to go out to play again, pretending I was off to do some hard graft and decision making. But on this particular Saturday I wanted to get home before cock crow and in the back of my mind there was still the niggling worry of the Crystal problem, which I knew was not going to go away. That was about as likely to happen as a politician owning up to a lie.

From Green Park I caught the last Victoria Line for Walthamstow where I had parked the Jag in a quiet street about a ten minute walk from the station. The car was parked near the end of a street where there was a long brick wall with a builder's yard behind it. I often chose to park there so as not to upset residents by parking outside their houses, even though they had no more guaranteed rights to park outside their homes than me. But I wasn't just being kind and considerate. Once upon a dreary wet night I had parked in a small residential area, and two neighbours had ganged up on me and my car was hemmed in front and back. It took me a good fifteen minutes and much cursing to get out of that tight spot as my car steamed up along with my temper. But that was nothing to the tight spot I found myself in as I reached what I thought was the safety of my car. I had just stepped off the kerb and walked round to the driver's side when dazzling headlights caught me in their glare like the flash from a camera, exposing my vulnerability. A sudden accelerated roar as the car, a large Mitsubishi four-by-four, shot alongside and screeched to a halt just in front of my Jag, passing so close I had to squeeze myself tight against the car door to avoid being squashed and having my feet crushed. Doors rattled and squeaked open, then two threatening shadows stepped smartly out of the front of their vehicle, and a giant of a bloke struggled out of the back seat on the driver's side and waddled towards me around the back of their car. But the thug from the front passenger seat was the first to get to me and I braced myself for the attack. His left hand grabbed my jacket lapels and squeezed hard, pulling me forwards ready for the punch with his right.

'Wait a minute!' I said. 'We can talk about this.'

But by now the lumbering giant had reached me and his enormous hands grabbed my shoulders and hurled me round so that I was pinioned against my Jag with my back to my attackers. His weight pressed against me and I could smell his rancid sweat and stale odour of too much tobacco. One of them hissed close to my ear, covering the side of my face with a stream of spittle.

'We have a proposition to give you from our boss. You know Dave Crystal, don't you?'

'I've heard of him,' I said. 'But I've never had the pleasure.'

Maybe it was the wrong thing to say, because a fist slammed into the small of my back. The pain was unbelievably intense, like a hammer hitting my body, and hot and cold needles of pain shot up my spine as I struggled to take a breath.

'Don't get smart with us, you fucking wanker. Our boss has heard how you made his nephew redundant, and Dave ain't too happy about that. So you better give him his job back.'

'And what happens if I don't?'

'You'd better like hospital food, cos you'll be eating it for a long while if you don't agree to Dave Crystal's proposition. You follow me?'

Stupidly, I said, 'I'm not sure that I do. A proposition is when you offer someone a choice which they can either accept or not.'

'Well, you ain't got any choice you smart-arsed cunt.'

The thug who had done all the talking squeezed his fingers around the back of my neck and pressed my head on to the roof of my car so that my face was squashed hard against the metal. This was followed by a searing pain in my kidneys as the fat monster jabbed a rock-hard fist into my back.

I cried out in pain, a guttural sound that I hoped would wake the neighbourhood. Maybe the three thugs worried about the volume of noise the pain had provoked from the depths of my gut, and they released their grip on me. Even though I was struggling to stay on my feet and trying to cope with the pain that was surging through my body like a wave with spikes on it, I got the impression they were easing back to the safety of their car, keen to be on their way in case someone phoned the police.

The driver of the vehicle spoke for the first time. 'Does Bob Crystal get his job back or do we have to come and find you to rearrange your face?'

I rubbed my back, trying to ease the pain, praying there was no damage to my kidneys.

'Well?' the driver insisted. 'You gonna give him his job back or we gonna come back and show you what real pain feels like?'

'OK,' I croaked. 'He gets his job back. He'll be back on the doors on Tuesday.'

'What's wrong with Monday?'

'The club's shut on Monday.'

'You better not be lying.'

'I'm not. We occasionally have private functions on a Monday – but this Monday there's nothing going on. We're shut.'

The driver cleared his throat noisily before speaking, making it sound like an exclamation of contempt. 'OK, so you'd better see Bob Crystal's back on the door by Tuesday night – or I'd hate to be in your shoes if he's not.'

'Don't worry,' I said. 'He'll be there.'

They seemed satisfied with this false promise and got back in their car, slamming the doors noisily. They sped off and were at the end of the road in seconds. I watched as the brake lights of their Mitsubishi shone brightly before it screeched round the corner out of sight, followed by a squeal of burning rubber.

I breathed slowly and gently, waiting for the sharp pain to subside. It was like I had swallowed a stone that was lodged in my stomach, a severe constipated feeling. But at least I knew that it was a warning and had they really gone to town on roughing me up, I wouldn't have been upright. I fumbled for my car keys, clicked open the door, and eased myself into the seat, feeling a sharp stab of pain in the guts as I shifted. I sat back and waited, taking things easy, waiting for some sort of speedy and miraculous recovery, while I thought about the alarming events, wondering how the hell they had found me.

On the previous night I had also left a bit earlier than usual and caught a train at just gone half past midnight from Green Park. So maybe Dave Crystal had me followed. I hadn't noticed anything suspicious, but then there were plenty of late night revellers in the carriage back to Walthamstow, it being a Friday night, so I wouldn't have noticed anyone following me. Even on the ten minute walk to my parking space I hadn't paid any attention to footsteps dogging mine as there were many late night stragglers staggering home well-bladdered after a night on the sauce.

And then something clicked in my head. A grey or silver Mitsubishi four-by-four, which I hadn't registered at the time, had been parked near Walthamstow Tube station when I came out of there just ten minutes ago. I hadn't really noticed it because there must have been at least a dozen illegally parked vehicles, as there usually were late at night when the traffic wardens are all tucked up in bed. So when I came out of the station, they must have seen where I was heading, having tailed me the previous night, and then followed me slowly at a distance.

I sat behind the wheel of my Jag for a long while, the internal pain in my back worryingly sharp, and I hoped that when I arrived home and used the loo I wouldn't see a stream of blood in my piss. But that would eventually heal and was nothing to the horror of what Crystal's mob were likely to do to me should I not reinstate his nephew. I was aware my life was in danger, because a severe beating could go badly wrong and turn into manslaughter. Maybe it was the pain, or perhaps it was the morbid thoughts of how my life had suddenly escalated into a disaster zone, but I felt tears bursting into my eyes and impairing my vision. I wiped them away with my hand, worried in case the sickly dread of self-pity and fear would stop me from making the right decisions. Decisions. Choices. Who was I trying to fool? I didn't have any choices. I saw neon signs in my head shouting NO OPTIONS. There seemed to be no way out of this mess. I was stuck up shit creek.

And for what? Because some crummy gangster had been barred from a club. As I thought about the injustice of it, the sheer stupidity and absurdity of it, I felt tears rising to the surface again.

Life had been good. No, change that to great. I was screwing a decent living, and things were ticking by with no major complications. I had lived a carefree life over the last couple of years, with very few problems. Just the usual headaches employers have with staff, but nothing mega.

And now, out of the blue, I had a vicious thug like Dave Crystal on my back. A psychopath. And by all accounts the entire family was mental and needed locking up and chucking away the keys. So there was no way I could reinstate Bob Crystal at the Velvet. And Sean had made sure he wouldn't be allowed back on the premises. I was well and truly painted into a corner and had until Tuesday to come up with a plan.

Two days to think of something. But what? My mind was a blank.

9
THE STING

Sunday was a dull day, cold with sombre grey clouds covering London like a blanket of depression, jeering at me, adding to my self-pitying gloom. The only bit of brightness on the horizon was the fact that when I arrived home in the early hours and visited the loo, I saw that my urine was typically amber in colour, as it usually was on a Saturday night after excessive boozing, but at least it ran free of blood. My kidneys seemed to have survived the beating, in spite of the intermittent twinges of pain in that area.

I showered for longer than usual, kidding myself that the torrent of water had healing properties, but when I stepped out of the shower cabinet on to the bathmat, I felt a stab of pain in the small of my back, gritted my teeth, and crossed my fingers I could walk normally when I got downstairs. I didn't want to alarm the family and I hoped I could fake the occasional spasm as a hangover instead of a thrashing – which would mean a tongue lashing from Michelle about driving under the influence, but there was no way I was going to worry them with thoughts of losing a husband and father because a spiteful gangster was barred from a club.

As I entered the kitchen, wearing black denims and a pale blue T-shirt, I managed to ignore the twinges in my abdomen and slid a chair away from the table. The loud scraping noise of the wood on the ceramic tiles set my teeth on edge.

'Freddie!' Michelle rebuked me as she unloaded the dishwasher. 'You're always telling the girls off about being too lazy to lift the chairs.'

Luckily she had her back to me and didn't see my grimace of pain as I slid into my seat. 'Sorry, sweetheart, I forgot.'

She glanced over her shoulder, a suspicious look through narrowed eyes. 'Have you been drinking too much again?'

'I may have had a few, but I was all right to drive, I promise.'

'So why d'you look so rough?' she demanded as she turned her attention back to the dishwasher and unloaded the few remaining plates.

'I felt peckish when I got to Walthamstow and had a kebab. It's given me the guts ache.'

She stood up straight, shut the dishwasher and turned to face me. I was relieved to see her laughing.

'Not a doner kebab?'

I nodded sheepishly.

'And you have the cheek to lecture your children about junk food. The man who is so sanctimonious about food. The foodie who won't let anyone enjoy an occasional guilty pleasure, goes out and stuffs himself with...'

I laughed, playing along with her taunting routine. 'Enough already! It was a mistake. Not one I will repeat, I can assure you.'

Whenever we go into this sort of double-act, I know things are OK between us and I wondered why everything was suddenly so satisfactory. She seemed to have forgotten all about our conversation concerning Dave Crystal and the threats to my well-being. So I guessed there must have been some sort of domestic improvement on the Jackie front.

'Talking of junk food,' I said. 'How's Jackie?'

She spread her arms in a gesture of appeal. 'Oh, come on, Freddie, you know that's not true. On the whole, Jackie's got a very good diet.'

'Sorry. I was just being flippant. So how is she?'

'She's fine. In fact, she's more than fine. No longer the stroppy teenager. She was all sweetness and light this morning, and after breakfast she went back upstairs – to 'mix some sounds' she said. And when I asked her to do it quietly, because you were still in bed, she agreed without a murmur.'

'You don't suppose...' I began, but Michelle was ahead of me and answered before I could finish.

'I think she might have heard about him getting his fingers broken. Yes.'

'And it's cheered her up?'

'Probably. Well… let's face it… he treated her appallingly. The wanker!'

I grinned at Michelle. 'Perfect description of the bloke. Now let's hope Jackie has learnt something from the incident and we can all settle down and get on with life as normal.'

An involuntary icy shiver rippled up and down my spine as I was reminded of my predicament, and I wondered if Michelle noticed, because she came over and kissed the side of my head.

'In the end,' she whispered, tenderly caressing my cheek, 'as far as Jackie's concerned, maybe it's all turned out for the best.'

I realised she hadn't noticed my nervousness and was forgiving me for taking revenge on behalf of my daughter, an incident that she would see as having worked out well for the family. And the family was the most important consideration.

On my way downstairs I had heard the sound of the television coming from the lounge. 'Olivia watching TV?' I asked.

'Yes. I'm about to take them both swimming. I don't suppose…'

I shook my head. Michelle knows I can't stand public swimming pools with chlorine clutching you like warm bleach. Give me an outdoor pool in a hot climate any day.

'I'll do the Sunday dinner,' was my excuse.

After Michelle and the girls had gone, I suspected the discomfort in my stomach was hunger pain as much as the beating, and I staggered to my feet and made a *cafetiére* of strong coffee, scrambled eggs, toast and smoked salmon. After I'd eaten, I began to feel a bit more human, although the occasional twinge in my stomach was a reminder of what my future would be like if didn't comply with Uncle Psycho's instructions.

After smothering a leg of lamb in honey and mustard, and putting it in the oven to cook slowly over the next three hours, I opened a bottle of Mouton Cadet, poured myself a glass and took it through to the lounge. I switched the TV on and zapped through the channels until I found something worth watching. I found a film that had just started on one of the Freeview channels, the familiar Scott Joplin tune setting the scene as *The Sting* began. Of course, I'd seen the film before, when it was first released, but it was one I remembered enjoying. Even though my brain was still in shreds and I found it difficult to concentrate, I settled back to watch it, only half paying attention, my thoughts random and scattered. Perhaps it was because of the way my mind was soothed by the piano, which I found relaxing and slightly soporific, but there flashed forward an image in my head of how the film ended, and I remembered from all those years ago the brilliant sting towards the closing moments when they actually built a false betting shop in order to scam the Robert Shaw character.

And that was when my mind changed gear, becoming unexpectedly alert as I made the connection between the plot of the film and my dodgy predicament. At first I thought I might just be focusing on one of those futile ideas that desperation brings to the surface but is really a pathetic attempt at survival, with no basis for an intelligent result. On the other hand, it was an idea, and any idea was better than none. And it might just work, I told myself. Eureka!

I sipped the wine, which was smooth and luscious, and I began to feel a glow as I thought about what I needed to do. I would need to contact Jack and Sean as soon as possible, to see if they were willing to help me out. My plan might just appeal to Sean, although as manager he might not be able to wholeheartedly approve of my plot. But I could also ask Harvey Costigan, who was the owner of the Liquid Velvet, if he would back me up.

I turned the volume low on the TV and reached for the cordless to make the calls. If they all agreed, the plan might just work. But it also meant I had to visit Uncle Psycho himself to see if I could con him into believing he could take his revenge in another way. And that, I realised, would be the hard part of the plot. Jumping into that snake pit, into the clutches of a mad bastard who liked nothing better than torturing small helpless creatures, would be more dangerous than some of my mercenary exploits. If this went wrong, I was a dead man walking.

10
VIP NIGHT

After making four exploratory phone calls on Monday morning I eventually managed to locate Dave Crystal's hangout to an office in Camberwell above a tanning parlour called Sunbed Ritzy. The entrance to his office was in a side street and there was a speakerphone entry system, in front of which I hesitated before pressing the buzzer.

To say I was scared would be an understatement. If the gangster didn't fall for my plan and take me up on my offer and still insisted on his nephew being reinstated at the Velvet, then I was looking at nothing left to do other than pray for a miracle. But this was my only option and fortunately I now had help from Jack – and Sean and Harvey Costigan had also leant their support, knowing how desperate I was to stay alive and in one piece.

Mind you, it was going to cost me well over two grand, a sum which brought tears of rage to my eyes, but if I was to survive this trauma, I was going to have to keep the anger in check and not let Crystal rile me.

I had to give an Oscar-winning performance. Be calm, keep cool and don't let him think for a minute that you're planning anything underhand. I went through any last minute scraps of dialogue in my head, took a deep breath and pressed the buzzer. I felt tension like bile rising in my throat. After a moment, a rasping, snarling voice came on the speakerphone.

'Who is it?'

'It's Freddie Weston to see Dave Crystal.'

A long pause. Clearly my unexpected visit had thrown confusion into the works. Eventually, the snarling voice ordered me to the first floor, and the door latch buzzed. I pushed it open quickly and stepped inside the gloomy hallway leading to stairs with threadbare carpeting then let the door swing shut on its spring. I was plunged into darkness and my fear returned like a bad dream, my breaths were short and shallow, and my legs felt as if they were weighted with lead as I climbed the stairs. As I reached the landing on the first floor, the door was flung open and the overweight man, the bloke who was responsible for my near kidney failure, filled the space like a monster in a presentation box.

'What do *you* want?' he demanded.

As I approached, I cleared my throat softly before speaking. 'I need to speak with Mr Crystal.'

From inside the office, a voice – which sounded like the Dalek voice from the speakerphone – said, 'Show him in, Trunky.'

The rotund monster moved aside, sending out a sickly sweet splash-it-all-over smell of aftershave as I squeezed past him into a large, spacious office. Seated behind a huge desk was the man himself. I had never set eyes on Dave Crystal before, and I was surprised to discover a small man with silver hair, round and daintily cherub-like but with paper-thin lips, in a face that was surprisingly unlined and boyish, even though I knew he was in his mid-fifties. But if his face was youthful, the eyes revealed a self-satisfied smugness and an indifference to cruelty. It was like staring into a dead pool, polluted by evil thoughts. But the lack of lustre in his eyes was spiced up by his blue suit which radiated a neon funfair glow.

I broke eye contact with him and glanced around the office. There were the usual black-and-white framed photographs on the walls of classic boxing matches that appeal to sporting types, even below-the-belt ones like Crystal. There were no filing cabinets in the office, but dominating a green pistachio-coloured wall was a hideous cocktail cabinet, glittering gilt edges and garishly decorated plastic, so tasteless I wondered if it was making some sort of ironic statement. A silver laptop was open on his desk and there was a telephone next to it. No paper, notebooks, pens or pencils. But there were at least half a dozen mobile phones that looked brand new. Probably pay-as-you-go to avoid being traced. I didn't think this office did much in the way of legitimate business. It was a hideout, from where he ran his dirty business.

From what I'd heard about the Crystal organisation, their trade was mainly in prostitution and loan sharking, and I also learnt they had recently expanded into human trafficking. But no drugs. They had wisely left that market to the black gangs that dominated many of the south London districts.

I was just wondering what my first move would be when Crystal's sandpaper voice reminded me how vulnerable I was.

'Fuckin' cheek coming here uninvited. I hope it ain't to tell me Bob ain't got a fuckin' job no more.'

'Not exactly,' I said, knowing once I'd launched my plan I would have no option but to go through with it, and get my message over quickly to capture his attention before he let his gorilla loose on me. 'I've really come to see you on behalf of the Liquid Velvet, who now regrets having barred you from the premises.'

His eyes narrowed. 'Now why would a West End club give a fuck about barring me?'

It was the question I'd been dreading. I wasn't dealing with a complete simpleton and I had to make it convincing.

'Because they know of your reputation. They know they're dealing with someone to be reckoned with. And they want to patch things up.'

'Well, they've got every opportunity of doing that.' His eyes blazed and he banged a fist on the desk. 'By giving my nephew his fucking job back. And if you've come here to tell me something different…'

I raised my hand. 'Listen, Dave – I hope you don't mind if I call you Dave – I've spoken to the manager of the club – and the owner – and they sincerely regret what happened, so they'd like to invite you back to a private VIP do in three weeks' time. Everyone who's anyone will be there.'

'Oh, yeah? And why exactly will they be inviting me to rub shoulders with London's finest?'

A trickle of sweat ran from under my left arm and I regretted wearing a leather coat. 'Like I said, they know of your reputation, and they don't want to mess with you. Clubs thrive on customers like yourself and they deeply regret what happened.' I placed a hand on my pounding heart to show how sincere I was. 'And I'll be honest, Dave, the reason they don't want to mess with you is cos they're scared of what you might do. Especially…'

I let the carrot dangle and he picked up the cue.

'Especially?'

'Especially as they know that Bob Crystal freaked out and half-killed a bloke when something snapped in his head. They daren't risk him doing the same thing at the Velvet.'

'How the fuck do they know about Bob's little… mistake?'

'Because I told them. One of my doormen was doing a stretch at Maidstone and he recognised him, and pretty soon we had the full SP. Now the club have sent me along to ask you to be reasonable and they're willing to welcome you back to the club by inviting you to this special do.'

Crystal sneered. 'Supposing I don't want to go to the fucking club? Supposing I feel that fucking insulted I might just tell the cunts go fuck themselves?'

He looked round at his Incredible Hulk and I thought he was going to issue orders to have me worked over again.

'Listen!' I said hurriedly, this time going for broke. 'You must have known at Bob's trial what he was like. And if Bob's old man gets to hear of you setting him up, placing him in a position where he might seriously damage a club punter and get himself put away – next time for life, maybe – your brother wouldn't be too pleased. I mean – and I'm only guessing here – you must get on OK with your brother and nephew. What do you think would happen if your brother found out you'd set his son up and were responsible for having him put away for life?'

I was skating on ice so thin it was like rice paper. I had threatened Crystal and he wasn't going to like it. The only thing left now was to appeal to his sense of drama and the way he could get his petty revenge.

'Which is why,' I said hurriedly, 'the club wants you on their side and have invited you to this do. There are certain conditions, of course.'

'Conditions!' Crystal suddenly shouted. 'What fucking conditions?

I gave an ever so humble apologetic shrug. 'Well, you know –'

'No, I don't fucking know!'

'Your language and behaviour, which got you barred, was far from acceptable, so the owner and manager sent me to invite you to this VIP do and asked me to plead with you to be on your best behaviour. Because if you don't…'

I stopped speaking, letting it sound like the start of a threat. Sure enough, he leant forwards, his eyes locked with mine and I felt an icy tingle of fear at the back of my neck.

'Yeah? And what will happen if I don't behave my fucking self?'

'Nothing. Well, not to you. But if there's a repeat of what got you barred from the club, it could have serious repercussions for them. The people who'll be attending spend a small fortune there, and if they lose that custom it would have a domino effect and the trade could be damaged beyond repair. They might never recover. This is one of the most prestigious events in the Sloane Ranger swank calendar and it needs to go off without a hitch. Jesus! They'll all be there. There's even a lord who's sixteenth in line to the throne. Which is why they've asked me to beg you to be on your best behaviour.'

As I watched him mulling this over, the tension in the office rose like a thermometer dipped in boiling water. His hand balled into a fist, but it was only to tug at his nose with a finger and thumb. I glanced at his bodyguard, who wore a slight smile, as if he hoped his boss would find my offer unacceptable. I wondered where the other blokes were, the ones who had helped to rough me up on Saturday night. Probably out putting the frighteners on the poor bastards who owed this outfit money. I hoped they weren't due back soon. Not that I fancied my chances with the Hulk, but at least I knew I could move quicker than him if it came to the crunch. Then again, Dave Crystal didn't get where he is today by fighting fair, and I suspected that if this confrontation turned nasty he was the sort of bloke who could instantly lay his hands on a weapon or two.

I saw Crystal lean back in his chair, fixing me in his sights like I was a target.

'Let me get this straight. You supply the doormen for this poncey club, and they've told you they don't want Bob on the door. But suddenly they do a complete about-turn and are happy to welcome me and my boys back into the club. Not only that, they're inviting me to hobnob with the cream of London society. Now this makes me suspicious, very suspicious indeed. It don't make no sense. What do you think, Trunky?'

A rumble of throaty laughter from the Hulk before he spoke. 'Don't make no sense at all, boss.'

I already knew Crystal wasn't going to fall for it that easily, so now I had to inject star quality into my performance. I placed a hand over my heart again, hoping it was not overdone, and gave him an almost tearful stare.

'It makes perfect sense. I can't tell you how much I had to beg the owner and the manager to help me out of this tight spot. Which is why I've come to you now with this offer. I'm the intermediary in all this and I'm just guessing that you hated being barred from the club – that sort of thing can damage your ego if word gets about – and so I got them to agree that providing we let bygones be bygones and I can talk with you… beg you… plead with you… to start afresh and behave yourself, then we are all winners, and there are no losers in this. We all come out of it with our pride intact, and I can breathe easy. And they're happy at the Velvet because they've got someone – to put it bluntly – someone they're shit scared of on their side. In fact – and I hope you won't take this the wrong way – one of my most persuasive arguments was to raise your reputation and profile as a lawbreaker, and we all know how much celebrities like to mix with people like you. Look at all the celebs who knocked around with Reggie and Ronnie. And the owner of the Velvet thought, as long as you and your boys behave like gents, then he sees it as a positive move for his club. And if these VIPs know who they're mixing with in three weeks' time, they'll come flocking back to the club on a regular basis. That's providing there's no repeat of the barring behaviour, of course.'

As I dished out this final ruling, I spotted the evil glint in his eye, and he could hardly disguise a nasty smile tugging at the corners of his mean thin lips.

And I knew, beyond a reasonable doubt, that Dave Crystal intended to be on his worst behaviour at the Velvet three weeks today.

But after these long speeches I felt drained. And thirsty. I needed to throw an ice cold lager down me. Quench my thirst along with my fear. I heard a car's pounding stereo from outside, thudding like the beat of my heart, and I longed for the sanity of the litter-strewn streets below. Eventually, Crystal nodded his head ever so slowly before he spoke.

'So what happens now? Me and the boys just turn up on the night?'

I let my breath out slowly. The man had bought it. I could have punched the air jubilantly, but I restrained myself and kept my expression neutral and businesslike.

'As it's a private do, I'll get the club to issue you with invitations. Shall I tell them to send it to this address?'

'No reason why not. And we need eight invitations, for my boys and all our other halves.'

I nodded an agreement. 'Eight invites it is. See you three weeks today then.'

I turned to take my leave, nodded to the Hulk, whose lower lip was prominently sulky, like a child deprived of a treat, now that he no longer had a reason to batter me to a pulp.

'Just a minute!' Crystal said.

I turned in the doorway to face him and I wondered if he'd smelt the proverbial.

'What is it?'

'My nephew Bob. Maybe he can't work at the Liquid Velvet, but if you want me to forget his sacking from the club…'

'Not exactly a sacking,' I said.

I shrugged and turned my hands over, a futile but small gesture of my compliance. And then the Hulk, robbed of his physical recreation, said, 'If he says it's a sacking, it's a fucking sacking.'

'D'you mind if I ask you something?' I said. 'What sort of moisturiser do you use?'

The Hulk's jaw flopped open in confusion, but his boss banged the desk again with his fist.

'You trying to be funny, cunt?' He gave me the hard, between-the-eyes stare. *Don't fuck with* me, *sunshine*. 'I've been very – how shall I put it? – generous in letting you off the hook and agreeing to attend this function these fuckers are holding, but I can't let my nephew down. So if he can't work at the Liquid Velvet, what's he going to do for employment?'

How stupid could I have been? My smart-arse line directed at his henchman hadn't exactly been side-splitting but it was enough to draw attention to the fact that I might be pulling a fast one. Now Crystal wanted to prove he had supreme power and would make greater demands. And I could see the way his mind worked. With Bob Crystal installed at another of my venues, the bastard hoped he might still freak out and injure someone, thus discrediting me. I should learn to keep my mouth shut.

'Don't worry, Dave,' I said. 'I'll give Bob work at another of my venues. I've got just the place. Somewhere where they don't know about his little… mistake.'

His eyes narrowed. Echoing his words like that was pushing my luck and he wasn't sure whether I was taking the piss or not.

'So where's this other club you're putting my nephew to work?'

'Kismet.'

'Never heard of it.'

'It's owned by Mark Lennox.'

Crystal nodded thoughtfully. 'Yeah, I know him. Met him a few times. Never liked the cunt. But he's got a lot of clout in certain areas.'

'And he's ploughing a load of money into the Kismet,' I said, injecting enthusiasm into my tone. 'It should go places, and soon be on the up-and-up given time.'

I caught the evil glint in his eye as I said it. I could see the way his dirty conniving mind worked. If by getting his nephew to work at the Kismet, who might freak out some day, not only would it damage me, but it would crucify Lennox as well. Not that that bothered me, but I didn't want to be the cause of an unsuspecting customer getting beaten half to death. Or even worse – to death.

My only hope was that Lennox would soon have total control of the Kismet and Bob Crystal would be sacked by him and not me.

I decided it was time to leave.

'I'm glad that's sorted then. See you in three weeks. Have a nice day.'

I exited hurriedly, before they noticed the relief and the demeanour of a man who's just pulled a fucking good stroke.

11
THE HACK

For the next three weeks, although I had to make preparations for Crystal's event at the Liquid Velvet, I began to relax now I'd been let off the hook. I installed his nephew at the Kismet and, although the lad was a bit sniffy about the venue, at least he behaved in a professional manner and was always reasonably polite and composed. But I still had to keep reminding myself that, if he was pumping iron and on the steroids again, then he could go off on one at any moment. Luckily, I got a phone call from Mal telling me Lennox now owned the Kismet and he (Mal) had been given his marching orders and was about to retire to live in Spain. Not so lucky was Lennox phoning my mobile (Christ knows how he got my number) to tell me he would be employing my staff, including Bob Crystal, and there was fuck all I could do about it. It pissed me right off. But he was right – there was nothing I could do about it. And then I remembered Michelle's warning about the danger of Crystal harming a punter and I tried to warn Lennox.

'Listen,' I said. 'You're welcome to my staff, but I don't think you ought to employ Bob Crystal.'

'No, you listen,' his voice crackled. 'He works for me now and you can go and fuck yourself.'

And then he cut the call. So now I was torn between my good and bad conscience, not wanting Bob Crystal to freak out and injure one of the punters, but the bad part of me hoped he would go ape one night just to get back at Lennox.

The day Lennox phoned me, I happened to be at home, and Michelle heard my half of the conversation. After the call, when I pointed out my dilemma, we had another argument about the situation.

I tried to explain to her that I was really snookered because I couldn't take Crystal away from the Kismet without crossing swords with Lennox. Not only that, but the wicked uncle and his mob were likely to give me a savage pasting for breaking our agreement. But Michelle was in one of her hate the East End moods and her suburban Surrey disapproval saw no grey areas. As far as she was concerned, anyone born within a mile of bow bells was a vicious thug. Of course, in a way I could see her point. After all, I was up treading a fine line between respectable family man and life in the underworld. But, as I pointed out, I have to make a living in the only way I knew how. I also hinted strongly that she had done all right out of it over the years.

That did it! We had a screaming great row, and she stormed out of the house to visit one of her friends. That was when I called Alison — or Ali as she likes to be called — and we fixed up a dinner date.

Not that I intended sleeping with her to get back at Michelle. Dinner and a flirtation would be enough.

For now.

★

I chose an excellent Chinese restaurant I know, a restaurant I'd never taken Michelle to, near Marble Arch, and arrived ten minutes early. I ordered a Bombay gin and tonic, told them to forget the complimentary prawn crackers, and sat on a bench seat by a low table in the small bar area.

Ali arrived only five minutes after the time we said we'd meet and I could see she'd made an effort for our assignation by dressing in an expensive-looking black, tight-fitting dress, a sexy little number that showed off her contours. Her hair, too, looked like it had been recently coiffured in an exclusive Mayfair establishment. I began to think I was under dressed in my pale blue sweater and black cords, but then I often dress down when I'm just chasing new business, which is what I'd told Michelle I was up to.

'Sorry I'm late, Freddie,' she said as she slid into the seat next to me, and gave my arm a gentle squeeze.

I felt a slight tingle from her touch, a sensual warmth, the sort of feeling that vanishes with the old and familiar.

'At the risk of sounding sexist,' I said, 'five minutes is not late for someone of your gender. A drink to kick off with?'

'I'll just have a tomato juice for now, and stick to wine with dinner.'

While her drink was being poured, the cocktail pianist in the dining room began playing 'As Time Goes By.'

Ali giggled and said, 'Very romantic. Have you been here before, Freddie?'

'Once,' I said, knowing she was fishing to see if I'd been here with other women. 'But it was strictly business,' I added. Which was true.

After the waiter handed us two giant menus, a muffled but insistent ring came from between us. She looked panic stricken, fumbled in her handbag and removed her mobile, now horribly shrill against the sweeping *Casablanca* tune and sophisticated atmosphere.

'Will you excuse me, Freddie?' she said. 'This is an important call. To do with work. I'll be as quick as I can. Sorry about this.'

She rose hurriedly and went outside. She saw me watching her through the window, gave me a wave as she started speaking, and then moved out of sight, almost as if she didn't want me to lip read her conversation. It was only a call on a mobile, I thought. Nothing to get your knickers in a twist about. But she probably thought it was bad form to leave her mobile switched on as we were about to have dinner.

Then I noticed her handbag, open on the seat next to me, and I have to admit I was tempted. I'm a nosy, suspicious sort of a bloke, and I never trust what is handed to me on a plate. So, one eye on the window, I slid my hand into the bag and rummaged through the usual handbag detritus. I didn't look down but straight ahead, doing the search by touch alone. And then my hand felt a little square of smooth plastic in a leather case, what felt like an ID wallet. I pulled it out, keeping it hidden low, just in case she walked back into view. I turned the ID case over. I almost laughed aloud when I saw what it was. Although I was holding it a long way from my eyes, and

I sometimes have to use off-the-peg reading glasses, I'm long-sighted and it was no effort for me to see that it was a union membership card. She was a member of the National Union of Journalists. She was using her real first name, but had lied to me about her surname, which she had told me was Grant. The union card gave her name as Alison Berger. Now why would she lie about her occupation, I asked myself. And then I remembered her probing questions when we had first met, plying me with questions about villains I might know. It looked as if she was on the make, as if she was looking for a story. Perhaps she was a crime reporter and it was a slow news day. Whatever the reason, I decided I would play the innocent doorman who could give her a scoop about villains.

And then I smiled as an idea hit me. I slid her union card back in the bag and waited for her return.

★

The food was excellent and I tucked in heartily, but I noticed she picked at minuscule amounts while we made small talk, and guessed she was deliberately holding back from asking me obvious questions about crime. Eventually, her voice light and nonchalant, and so quiet that I had to strain to hear her above the sounds of Cole Porter coming from the piano, she fed me her opening gambit.

'So how are things in the world of tough guys?'

I pretended I couldn't hear her. 'Sorry?'

She became flustered and laughed nervously before repeating her question.

'One of the tough guys – an old mate of mine – is having problems,' I answered, noticing the way her eyes widened in anticipation.

'Problems with the law or other tough guys?

'Both. But this friend of mine's in Spain and I don't think I can talk about it.' I shrugged a half-hearted apology. 'Not these days, what with them having an extradition treaty.'

'Oh, this sounds fascinating. Now we're friends, and might become *close* friends, I'd love to hear all about it. And I promise – cross my heart – I won't tell a soul. No one. On my mother's life.'

Your mother's probably dead, I thought.

'Well,' I said, pulling a face to show how awkward it was to betray a confidence, 'Difficult to name names. He's an old mate who masterminded a robbery. A biggie. Probably the biggest ever in this country. And most of the gang got caught, but he didn't. So if this got out, I might be condemning him to a long stretch behind bars.'

'You don't think I'd tell anyone, do you?'

'You could tell the police for a start.'

'Why would I do that? And if I gossiped to someone in a pub, saying I know someone who knows someone who's a robber hiding in Spain, they'd think it was just Chinese whispers and probably wouldn't be believed.'

'Yeah, but suppose, just through talking to the wrong person, it got in the papers? Some investigative reporter might latch on to it.'

She gave me a funny look, uncertain and inquisitive, wondering if I'd guessed her occupation. For a moment I wondered if I'd gone too far, and mentioning the press might trigger something in her subconscious about the open handbag she'd left next to me.

'On the other hand,' I added, 'I don't suppose your local rag's going to take much notice. Where is it you live?'

'Hampton Wick.'

I chuckled, making a joke of it. 'Yeah, I don't suppose the *Hampton Wick Bugle* would listen to gossip like that. They're too busy holding the front page for the results of the biggest marrow grown on an allotment.'

She laughed, put down her fork and placed a hand over mine. 'Seriously, Freddie, you lead such an interesting life and I'd love to hear more. Most of the men I work with in the office lead such dull lives.'

She took her hand away, picked up her fork again, and ate a tiny portion of chicken in lemon sauce. Clearly she was using a softly, softly approach.

'In my line of business,' I said, 'there's never a dull moment. And I guess this mate of mine's sitting pretty, especially as the police think they've got all the culprits under lock and key.'

'How big was this robbery?'

'About fifty-something million.'

'Was this the one down in – where was it? – somewhere in Kent?'

I guessed she knew damn well where it was, could probably pinpoint its location accurately.

'It was a money holding depot in Tonbridge.'

She clicked her fingers. 'Ah yes – Tonbridge. Now I remember. It was in all the papers for months. And didn't they imprison someone abroad, in a North African country?'

'Yeah, Morocco, cos he was half Moroccan. But he was just one of the muppets who committed the robbery. My mate engineered the whole thing, and got away with a modest five million and opened a small bar. Nothing too lavish to draw attention to himself.'

'Wow! That sounds like exciting stuff. Like something out of a movie. How close are you to this man?'

'We've been mates for years. I usually see him once a year, I go out to Spain for a week, and we play a lot of golf.'

This much was true, and I decided it was time to use the hook. She thought she was fishing in my pond, but little did she know it was the other way round.

'As a matter of fact, I'm seeing him in a fortnight's time. My usual golfing expedition has come around.'

'I'd love to meet your friend.' Her eyes lit up, like she'd had a sudden brilliant idea. 'Hey! Guess what? I'm due some annual leave around that time. I'd love to…' She stopped speaking, knowing she was moving too fast, and being less than subtle. 'No, it's out of the question.'

'What is?'

'Me coming to Spain with you. Your friend wants to remain anonymous, and even though it doesn't matter what he's done – not to me anyway – it would be wrong of me to intrude on his privacy. Oh, but it's just that… I'd love to meet a really successful villain. Someone who got clean away with it.'

I frowned and stared thoughtfully at the tablecloth and the grains of rice that had spilt from my plate, as if I was deliberating on a hard decision.

'I tell you what I'll do,' I said. 'I'll have a word with my mate. Tell him you'd like to come out to meet him – and to be honest he's a bit of a woman's man.'

She giggled. 'And you're not, I suppose.'

'No – seriously – I'm not. Although it might seem like that from my meeting you like this.'

She could hardly contain her excitement now and wanted to get me back on track.

'Sorry. I interrupted you. You were saying.'

'Yeah, I'll have a word with my mate. If he says no, then I'm sorry there's no way I can take you to meet him. On the other hand, you never know.'

'So when are you going out there?'

'Fly out late morning on the twenty-first of May from Stansted.'

'Well, I think I could get the time off if your friend agrees.'

'If he agrees – and this is a big 'if' mind – you could catch a flight from Heathrow…'

'Why can't we fly together?'

'Because Michelle, my wife, can drop me at Stansted, and she's a very jealous woman. I'll meet you at Malaga airport and we can go to Marbella together.'

'That's if it works out, of course.'

'Let's hope it does.'

Of course it would. My fish was well and truly hooked. When this little trip was over she was in for a shock, and would probably be reduced to a second string reporter on births, deaths and marriages. Not that I would feel any sympathy for her, seeing as how she thought she was setting me up. Apart from which – and I was just guessing – she probably worked for one of the seamier tabloids, the sort of rag where they'll pull any stunt to get a story. Suddenly, I'd gone from finding her attractive when I first met her to thinking I'd sooner go to bed with a female sumo wrestler. Not that I'd really intended on sleeping with her. Like I said, just a flirtation, but even that would have become an effort once I knew what she did for a living and how she operated in the most devious way.

Scum, that's what they are. I've hated them ever since an old Scouse mate of mine who was at the Hillsborough fiasco, was questioned in his local pub about the tragedy by a *Sun* reporter pretending to be a sympathetic listener. Twisted words and dirty stories, that's what they're about, and if people like my Scouse mate gets trodden on, what does it matter? I hate them.

And helping to consolidate my distrust of that society of arseholes, Ali said, in what I thought was a wheedling manner, 'Please, please tell your friend he can trust me implicitly. And I swear nothing will escape these lips.'

I flashed her a broad smile, hoping my insincerity didn't show. 'Don't worry, Ali, I have a feeling this might work out. I'll give my mate a bell tomorrow and then I'll call you and let you know if it's on. Then you'll be in time to make flight arrangements.'

'I hope your friend doesn't say no. I'll be so disappointed now if he does.'

'We shall see tomorrow,' I said with slight hesitation, as if there still might be some doubt about the trip, but knowing full well it would be all systems go. This was just the sort of stunt I knew would appeal to Sid. Not only that, his wife and he split up six months ago, and I figured he might be up for some revealing pillow talk after a night of pleasure, whoever it was with.

12

THE STING II

When the big night of the private function at the Liquid Velvet arrived, I felt as nervous as hell. What if it went horribly wrong? What if Crystal recognised one of the elite guests as an extra from an episode of *EastEnders*? I thought it was highly unlikely, but I was worried that one of the wives or partners in his party might identify someone as a face they saw in the background of a scene at the Queen Vic pub. When I mentioned my concerns to Sean, he assured me I was worrying unduly because he thought Crystal and his mob would tank themselves up before making an appearance. No matter how confident the gangster thought he was, he said, Crystal would want to get himself well and truly oiled to enable him to cope with being looked down on as a lowlife oik by people he classed as snobby gits. I guessed Sean was right, but I still worried myself sick at the outcome of this 'sting' if it went wrong. But what choice did I have?

Crystal and his mob's specially cobbled invitations gave the start of the event as 8:30. Jack and I had arranged for our counterfeit upper-class revellers to arrive at 7:30 so that I could fill them in on how I guessed Crystal and his entourage would behave. Although I was on edge, I couldn't wait to see the gangster and his motley crew when they showed up, thinking they were about to rub shoulders with the Right Honourable Sir Gordon Willoughby and Lady Antonia Willoughby who were celebrating Miss Portia Willoughby's engagement to Mr Clive Petworth, a few names I'd made up for the invitations, hoping Crystal or one of his mob didn't do a Google search.

Jack had informed me that many background performers, in order to give them greater opportunities for work, can dress for most occasions, provided it is contemporary rather than costume drama – some can even supply their own police uniforms. So when I telephoned a walk-on agency he'd recommended and asked them if they could supply me with two dozen extras for a low budget film, dressed for an up-market function, some masquerading as aristocrats, they informed me it would be no problem, and offered to supply me with a dozen males of varying ages in dinner jackets, and a dozen females, also of varying ages, in cocktail dresses. I told the man at the agency it was just what I needed for the shoot, which would last only two or three hours, because I figured Crystal and his mob would by then be satisfied they had destroyed the reputation of the club. The agent told me if the shoot lasted only ten minutes instead of seven hours, the minimum daily rate of £105 per extra would still apply and he would need me to email him a work order. I made up some film company stationery on my computer and sent it off to him, hoping the extras he sent me would be reasonably believable.

When the first of my bogus guests arrived, I was surprised by how convincing they looked. Two men in immaculate dinner suits, both distinguished-looking, middle-aged with white hair, and a woman of around thirty, with a slender figure and a body-hugging red dress, fitted the bill perfectly. One of the men though had a wart-like growth on his forehead that my eyes were drawn to as I spoke to him, and I wondered if most directors kept this actor well into the background of any shots. Not that it mattered to me, as we were only pretending to shoot a film. The next bloke who turned up, a man of around fifty – which may also have been his waist measurement – wore an ill-fitting lounge suit, and made a beeline for the first three guests and proceeded to tell them jokes. I made a mental note to keep this man as far in the background as I could, away from the main action.

When the next extra arrived I had to stifle a laugh. She must have been in her eighties and actually wore a fox fur, something I don't remember seeing since my Nan's days when I was about six. I stared with disbelief at the dead fox's bushy tail on her left shoulder and the glass eyes in the head on her other shoulder, wondering if this was some sort of joke. I almost expected the fox to give me a conspiratorial wink. The evening was now becoming surreal and I decided she could join the overweight man towards the rear of the proceedings.

By 8:15 all two dozen extras had arrived, and I was pleased to note that, with the exception of my eccentric fox fur woman and my overweight life-and-soul joker, the majority could have fooled most people into thinking they were distinguished guests at a posh do, and I began to relax, praying that Sean was right about Crystal and his mob turning up drunk. Also present to make up the numbers was Michelle, looking radiant in an outfit that had cost me a second mortgage, and Sean's girlfriend and a few of his friends who were also in on the scam.

Once everyone was assembled in the main bar area, some sitting on bar stools, or just leaning against the bar, others sitting on the long banquettes near the dance floor, I cleared my throat ready to play director and make a speech.

'Ladies and gentlemen, could I have your attention please,' I began, as the murmurs died down and they all stared at me expectantly. 'Thank you for your participation in this unusual and unique way of shooting a feature film.' I pointed to several CCTV cameras. 'You will notice CCTV cameras in various locations. These have now been fitted with high definition cameras and we will begin shooting as soon as our actors arrive at 8:30. As long as they're not held up in traffic.' I gave a little laugh, preparing them for a wait, in case Crystal and co didn't show up until much later.

'Now, although these actors have been briefed, they'll be improvising the scene, and I want you to be upper-class partygoers who disapprove of their presence. As soon as they arrive, give them snooty looks, as if they've just crawled out of the sewers. And some of the things they say you may find shocking. So by all means behave as if you are shocked. They've not been given a script to learn, and we'll keep shooting for as long as it takes and see how the scene develops. Your reaction is very important. These actors are playing thugs, and their language will be appalling, but that's all part and parcel of the scene – shocking the aristocrats. Are any of you trained actors who'd like to get away early?'

Stroking her fox fur seductively, the ageing woman announced, 'Celia Leverton!' She made it sound as if I should have heard of her. 'I worked for many years at the Old Vic, and I once played Portia to Robert Atkins's Shylock, so I'm up for it.'

I didn't want to hurt the old dear's feelings, so I pointed to one of the cameras. 'If you don't mind, Celia, you are perfect for this shoot, and you'll be on that camera, in that corner of the room, so I don't want to risk losing you too early. What I'm after is a man and a woman, posing as a couple, to give me a convincing performance of how insulted they appear, and to storm out once the actors go too far in their bad behaviour.'

The man with the growth on his head raised a hand to get my attention, 'We can do it,' he said, indicating a top-heavy woman standing next to him. 'We've worked together in rep. And be nice to get away early.'

I nodded and gave them a smile. 'Fine. All I want you to do, once the actors go over the top with their bad language, is register your shock – perhaps apologise to another guest, and then leave hurriedly. Think you can do that?'

'No problem,' the woman said.

'Good.' I checked the time on my watch. It was 8:20. 'Soon waiters and waitresses will be bringing you glasses of red or white wine, or a glass of orange juice for those who don't drink alcohol. They'll also be serving canapés as we wait for the actors to show up, which will add a touch of realism to the scene. So just relax now, talk and mingle as you would in any party, and enjoy a drink and some grub.'

Like puppets having their strings pulled, they all reacted as one, turning in to face each other in two and threes, and began chatting. I noticed my fox fur and fat joker were closest to the entrance, so I went over to them.

'I'd like you to come with me, Celia' I said. 'Over to the other side of the room, where one of our cameras can pick you up.' I turned to the fat joker. 'What's your name?'

'Len.'

'You too, Len.'

They followed me as I weaved my way to the furthest side away from the entrance. I told them to stay in that area.

'By the way,' the fat joker said, 'what's this film called?'

'Get Out of Jail Free.'

He sniggered like a naughty schoolboy, and I guessed this was to herald a joke. 'I once went to prison for my beliefs,' he said. 'I *believed* the bank had sacked their security guards.'

I gave him a half-hearted grin. 'The old ones are the best, eh, Len? What do you do when you don't do walk-ons? Stand-ups?'

'Yeah, I've done a bit of comedy. Done loads of different acts. I'm in the Variety Artistes Federation. You name it, I've done it.'

'So what do you do now, when you're not doing extra work?' fox furs asked him.

'Balloon sculpture.'

'What's that?'

'You know, folding balloons into all sorts of animal shapes for kiddies.'

I excused myself and went over to speak with Michelle. The DJ started playing music, kicking off with Elton John's 'Rocket Man.' It had previously been agreed we would play fairly middle-of-the-road music. And waiters and waitresses appeared from the kitchen with trays of drinks and canapés and started to distribute the refreshments to our phoney guests.

Michelle squeezed my arm, kissed my cheek and whispered, 'Try not to worry, sweetheart. It'll be fine.'

'I hope so, Michelle. You've arranged what you're going to say with Sean?'

She laughed nervously. 'It's all arranged. I'm almost looking forward to it.'

'It's all right for you – this little caper's costing me well over two grand. We'll have to tighten our belts after this for a while.'

'It could be worse.'

'Yeah? I'd like to know how.'

'At least the club's providing the food and drink.'

'Yeah, that's big of them, seeing as this was another fine mess they got me into.'

Michelle squeezed my hand and grinned. 'Stop complaining. Anything's better than ending up in hospital. And if you're talking of saving money, why don't you forgo your Spanish trip.'

I gave her a mock aghast look. 'The flight's booked and paid for. And you know how difficult it is to get a refund from a budget airline. Any airline, come to that.'

Sean came over and spoke to us, his eyes bright with excitement. 'As soon as these morons arrive I'm going to have to give them a welcoming smile and do Basil Fawlty at his most obsequious.'

'That shouldn't be difficult for you, Sean, you must be used to it.'

'Cheeky bastard. But you know what really gets me about this. If it all works out, those arseholes are going to go away thinking they've ruined our trade, and they'll never know they've been had. Still, at least we'll have CCTV of the whole event from start to finish.'

'Which you'll never be able to use. Because if they find out they were taken in by this hoax, their damaged egos will lead to a revenge too horrible to consider.'

Sean's confidence suddenly evaporated. 'My God! I should never have agreed to this cockamamie scheme.'

A sudden commotion from the entrance and my head whipped round as if it was on a spring.

'Too late, Sean,' I said. 'They've arrived.'

The doors were thrown open like a challenge and Crystal strutted forwards, his peroxide wife or mistress attached to his arm. She was middle-aged, so on second thoughts I guessed she was probably his wife. Villains like Crystal, if they have a bit on the side, are always true to type and go for girls at least half their age. He was also true to type in his swaggering entrance, like the bad guy in a cowboy film barging into the saloon, and I could see he was spoiling for a fight, even before he'd become acclimatised to the sober atmosphere of the room. He was followed by the Hulk, who was accompanied by a woman so thin she looked anorexic, and I couldn't imagine how she survived beneath his weight without snapping like a twig. These two were followed by a short, wiry, middle-aged man, and I could hazard a guess that this little bloke, like my old mate Bill, was probably the toughest of the lot, making up in pain threshold what he lacked in stature. But, unlike Bill, there was nothing pleasant about his face which was ugly with hostility. Just behind him, and at least a foot taller, came an attractive dark-skinned brunette, who looked as if she might be from one of the Latin American countries, young and with a much more sophisticated demeanour than the rest of the bunch.

I waited for the other bloke and his partner to make an appearance, but they hadn't been included in the party, in spite of being given invitations. Maybe the other gang member was out settling scores, or perhaps waiting in the car outside, having to stay sober enough to drive his boss home.

I could see Sean had been right in his predictions about them arriving in an inebriated state. They all had the rigid appearance of drunks trying not to give the game away by swaying like trees in a high wind.

Sean darted forwards to greet them. 'So glad you could make it,' he gushed, grinning and gesturing as if Crystal had just dropped in for afternoon tea at Blenheim Palace.

'Oh, are you?' Crystal mocked him with an imitation posh voice, then reverted to his natural South London. 'I ain't drinking fucking wine like these wankers. Got something stronger?'

Sean waved the barman over and said, 'Please serve Mr Crystal and his guests with whatever they're drinking.' He grinned at Crystal. 'It's all on the house.'

Crystal nodded, and for a sinking moment I thought he might be taken in by Sean's act of reconciliation and might start behaving himself. But I was worrying unnecessarily because as soon as they had all got their drinks from the barman, Crystal turned to one of my fake guests and demanded, 'What you fucking looking at? You got a fucking problem?'

Not wanting to miss the fun, his short comrade, eyes sodden and red-rimmed from excessive alcohol, snarled like a caged animal. 'Look at 'em. They're all fucking staring at us. All of them. The cunts!'

'Tha's it. You tell 'em, Lenny boy,' Crystal's wife slurred, holding on to the bar for support.

Picture of stunned disbelief from the extras, who looked as if they had their arse cheeks clamped tight after a eating a dodgy curry. I know I'd directed them to look shocked, but their reaction seemed genuine. And, as instructed, the DJ turned the music down several notches to emphasise the offended stillness of the guests, and the waiters and waitresses suspended their duties and became statues as all frosty eyes stared at the mob of second-class citizens lined up at the bar.

And then Crystal's missus, clearly unnerved by the icy reception, suddenly slammed her brandy and Coke down on the bar and screamed like a harridan at one of the extras, 'What's your fucking problem? Eh? Something wrong with our company is there? Fucking snooty bitch.'

The poor extra's mouth twitched, a nervous tic, and her hand clutched her neck for comfort – or maybe she was trying to dislodge a canapé that had got stuck in her throat. If this was acting, maybe they ought to consider giving walk-on roles a Bafta award. But perhaps she wasn't acting, because even I had to admit that Crystal's wife would have stunned a wound-up *X Factor* audience into silence.

Crystal laughed loudly, delighted with the effect they were having. 'That's telling her, Mo.'

The man partnering the frightened extra, scowled and threw Crystal a disparaging look. Every single extra stared at Crystal and his mob with a mixture of shock and hostility which was just what I wanted. Some of them went overboard in registering disdain, but then they thought they had nothing to fear from what they had been told was a group of very convincing actors. I caught Kevin's eye who was standing watchfully in a dark corner of the club, ready to leap in if it looked like Crystal or one of his men were about to physically attack one of the extras. And Jack, my martial arts expert, had slipped in quietly through the double doors leading into the club, with Roger waiting at the far end of the bar. If things got out of hand, all I had to do was give them the nod. But I hoped it wouldn't come to that. I needed to avoid a physical confrontation for my plan to work.

Now it was Michelle and Sean's girlfriend's turn to advance the plot. Sean's girlfriend was an attractive woman called Sara, and she and Michelle moved to within earshot of the Crystal party and complained loudly to Sean.

'How dare you invite these people to this private function,' Sara said. 'Have you taken leave of your senses?'

'You can forget our custom in the future,' Michelle piped up.

I could see the sneering smile now on Crystal's evil phizog. His wife, leaning against the bar, sliding sideways and losing control, yelled, 'These people! Did you hear the way that snobby bitch said "These people?"'

The man with the growth on his head, fooled into thinking his big break had come and this might be a scene he could use on his showreel, took the large-breasted woman by the hand, dragged her towards the entrance and took up a favourable position from where he could deliver his exit line.

'I have never been so humiliated in my life,' he boomed. 'Disgraceful behaviour. Absolutely disgraceful.'

Not to be outdone, the woman next to him bellowed, 'Worse than disgraceful! Worse than disgraceful!'

As they started to leave, Crystal addressed the Hulk. 'See his fucking head, Trunky. I think that was the club unicorn.'

The Hulk guffawed dutifully before adding, 'Yeah, I wouldn't like to head-butt that bastard. All that pus in there.'

'Leave it out, Trunky,' the skinny woman said, pulling a face.

As the extras exited, there was no way the man with the growth couldn't have heard what was said, and I felt a bit sorry for him. Then Sean ran after them, apologising profusely. Moments later he came back, wringing his hands and making futile gestures.

'They and their friends are some of my best customers. We'll be ruined. Ruined!'

I could see the effect this had on Crystal, who actually rubbed his hands like Fagin before picking up his gin and tonic and knocking it back.

Now most of the extras began complaining, and someone yelled loudly: 'I've never heard such disgusting language.' They all began overacting like mad, knowing they had nothing to fear as this was all part of a film being shot.

Suddenly the fat joker weaved his way to the front of the crowd and pointed an accusing finger at Crystal, just as the music ended.

'You people should be ashamed of yourselves.'

You could almost hear the tumbleweed blowing across the dance floor. Then Crystal, recovering from the frosty silence, staggered forwards, chin jutting out, and faced the fat joker. 'What you gonna do about it, you fat cunt?'

The fat joker was momentarily at a loss, then, either from nerves or because he found the situation funny, he began giggling.

'What you fucking laughing at?' Crystal sneered.

The fat joker caught my eye and mouthed, 'Sorry.'

I could have killed him. He probably thought I was going to shout 'cut' so we could reshoot the scene. Fortunately, Crystal and his mob were so drunk it went over their heads. But I was still worried in case one of them smelt a rat.

I turned away from the fat joker and decided it was time to plead with Sean. 'Jesus, Sean! I'm sorry. They promised they'd be on their best behaviour. I swear.'

Sean picked up his cue, as we'd arranged. 'Yes, you stupid bastard. You've killed this club off good and proper. It'll take months – maybe years – for us to recover. We'll be well out of pocket you stupid fucking moron.'

'I've never heard such disgusting language,' Crystal said.

'Fucking awful, Dave,' his wife added.

Crystal suddenly lunged towards one of the waitresses holding a tray of canapés, swept his hand upwards and her tray went flying through the air. She screamed as delicacies of smoked salmon were scattered over a wide area and the tray hit the dance floor with a clang.

'The food's crap as well!' Crystal yelled. 'Let's get out of this fucking shithole.'

I caught a glimpse of the young brunette and she seemed shocked, probably wondering what she had done to deserve a boyfriend like 'Lenny boy' and his obnoxious companions. But maybe she was an illegal immigrant and he was her meal ticket.

They all followed Crystal towards the exit, swaying and lurching drunkenly. Jack held the door open for them.

'I hope he don't expect a tip,' Crystal's missus said.

Crystal looked up at Jack, swayed backwards, and recovered. 'I'll give him a tip. Find another fucking job. This place has had it.'

The club was deathly quiet as Crystal and his mob departed, all the extras wearing stunned, mouth-gaping expressions. I waited a moment until I thought the gangster and his thick scum had left the premises, then I gave Sean a big grin and shouted 'Cut!' All the extras broke into a spontaneous round of applause.

'Best bloody performance I've ever seen,' said one of the them. 'Who were those actors?'

'Thank you everyone,' I yelled above the sudden babble, 'that was brilliant. You all gave me exactly what I wanted.'

'Just the one take?' another one questioned.

'Yes, you're all free to go, but please stay and finish your drinks if you like.'

Michelle appeared at my side, kissed me and said, 'I think you're supposed to say it's a wrap.'

I grinned at her and lowered my voice. 'We weren't really shooting a film, you know.'

'Yes, but they don't know that.'

One of the extras, a middle-aged man with a moustache, approached me, bent over and flapped a trouser leg, drawing my attention to a stain just below the knee.

'Look at that. This tux has just been cleaned and one of your canapés caught me on the knee and has left its mark. It'll need dry cleaning again.'

'Sorry about that,' I said. 'The actor was improvising. I had no idea he was going to do that.' I took out my wallet and handed him a ten pound note. 'I think that should cover the damage.'

He seemed more than satisfied, thanked me and hurried away. Sean came up and patted my arm.

'Well done, dear boy. I have to admit I really enjoyed that. Especially his bag of a wife freaking out like that. What an embarrassment she must be to her old man.'

'I doubt it very much, Sean. Crystal's the sort of bloke to have double standards and wouldn't like to hear his wife cursing.'

Sean frowned. 'But I don't understand... why would...?'

'He probably told her she could go overboard, get pissed and behave badly,' I explained. 'It was a good excuse for her to let it all hang out.'

'I'm sure she enjoyed herself immensely. But I don't think she'll remember much of it by tomorrow.'

'Who cares about those scumbags. I've got them off my back. And Crystal thinks he's got his revenge and ruined your business. We can all sleep peacefully in our beds tonight.'

'But before we do, dear boy' Sean said, turning on the charm with a wide grin, 'I've booked dinner for four of us at The Ivy. Courtesy of Harvey, who feels a tad responsible for your ills, liked and admired your cunning little plan, and wants to give you a treat. I'll go and call us a cab. See you in the foyer in ten.'

After Sean had gone, Michelle congratulated me. 'Well done, Freddie. Just think, if you hadn't watched that old film…'

'I might be lying half dead in a hospital somewhere,' I said. 'But I think that's the last we'll see of Crystal and his gang.'

She pecked my cheeks. 'Thank God for that. I'll just visit the little girl's room before we go. See you in a minute.'

'Yes, I'll meet you in the foyer.'

'I'm starving now,' she called over her shoulder as she went.

I was hungry too, but I suddenly felt extremely tired. I hadn't realised just how tense my body was. It had been an ordeal for me, wondering whether my cunning plan would work or not, and now my muscles felt weakened by the sudden release from nervous tension. I would sleep well tonight. Better than I had for weeks now my troubles were over. I could relax and enjoy my trip to Spain in only three days' time. But a lot can happen in three days. And not always for the best.

13
PROOF

I knew something was up as soon as Mum phoned me on my mobile wanting to know if Michelle was at home. She rarely called my mobile, so I suspected she had something important to tell me, something she didn't want Michelle to know. After a reluctant hesitation on my part, she repeated her question, and I assured her that Michelle had gone to pick up Olivia from school. When I asked her what was wrong, she said she wanted to see me in private, was sorry for being so secretive and had some important information for me. She sounded tearful and I wondered how much she'd had to drink, although she spoke quite coherently. So I left a note for Michelle, telling her where I'd gone – said I would get back as soon as I could – and drove over to see Mum in her small terrace house in the cul-de-sac in East Ham where I'd grown up.

It's strange how this small street of only seven houses on either side hasn't changed over the years and brings back many vivid memories whenever I visit. I often wonder how it never crossed my mind about our limited space when I was a boy. Being the youngest in the family, I was the one with the smallest of three bedrooms, which was more of a box room the size of a prison cell, but at least it was home, and to begin with, for the first ten years of my life, I remember it as a happy place. Which was the old man's doing mainly. He was so full of quick-fire wit, sharp with his answers and banter, and always kept us entertained with his humorous observations. Until he killed himself, and then he killed something in all of us. It was never the same after that.

The street had changed inasmuch as at least six houses were Asian owned, all the old East-enders having either died or moved to pastures new, but the street had retained its quaint respectability and tidiness, all the tenants proud of their small enclave in what had become a noisy, litter-strewn part of East London. The biggest change since I was a kid was what most residents considered an improvement – the installation of double-glazed windows. Even Mum had succumbed to this eighties trend, when cold-calling salesmen pestered and made a killing, some of them above board, others not so scrupulous. Fortunately for Mum, she had gone for one of the larger more reputable firms who advertised constantly on TV.

I managed to squeeze into a resident's parking space. Mum has never learnt to drive, but I've always paid for a parking permit which she's entitled to, so there's never any problem parking when I visit.

I have a key to the house, which is necessary because of Mum's age, and I dread the day when I can't get her on the phone and have to let myself in knowing she'll be dead. It was something I dreaded, but it was inevitable, unless she became too feeble to manage living on her own and had to go into a home.

As I let myself in, I called out, 'It's me, Mum!'

'In the back room, Freddie.'

There are two steps down into the back room, and I always have to duck as I enter, something I sometimes forget to do, because I never had to when I was a nipper. I was quite short and didn't grow to average height until I was sixteen or seventeen, and by then I was ready to enlist and leave home.

Mum looked up as I entered and right away I could tell by the redness in her eyes she'd been crying. She sat at the square dining room table, and I was surprised not to find a bottle and glass in front of her. But on the table to her right sat an old battered brown suitcase, the top open, and I could see it was filled with letters, mementoes and photographs. On the table next to it lay a magnifying glass.

The room always has a musty, familiar smell, which might be something to do with Mum's age, but there was also a faint odour of lavender, as if she'd been cleaning, perhaps to take her mind off what it was she wanted to share with me. Beyond the back room is a small kitchen extension with just enough room for a cooker, fridge, washing machine, small sink and draining board. As space was at a premium, the food cupboard had been built into the back room between the window and door leading to the kitchen. My eyes flitted about the room, and for a moment they focused on the fireplace with its beige-tiled mantelpiece and surround, a familiar feature I had accepted when I was a kid, but when I got older my tastes altered and I marvelled at its ugliness. I scanned the built-in dresser in the alcove next to it, searching for the inevitable bottle, always in evidence whenever I called round. But there was no bottle or glass on the dresser, or anywhere else in the room, and this made me suspicious as the drink was always there whenever I visited, boldly staring me in the face, because Mum couldn't give a monkeys what I or anyone thought. My eyes were drawn to the kitchen and I looked towards the sink, squinting at the evidence I had almost missed, there on the draining board. A tumbler upside down on it, perhaps hastily rinsed out before my arrival. Finding this deeply disturbing, I bit hard on my bottom lip. Mum has always drunk openly and told me to go to hell when I complained about it, but if she'd now taken to burying the evidence, it was a worry. I didn't like to think of her shamefully hiding booze from me, and I worried about just how much she was secretly putting away.

'Stop nosing around, Freddie, and sit yourself down.'

She knew I was searching for signs of alcohol.

'Can I get you anything before I start?'

I shook my head. 'I'm all right.' I knew this was an excuse – if she offered me a drink she could have one herself. Now she was playing the respectable drinker. I'll have one if you're having one, just to keep you company. I've known several alcoholics in my time, and I recognised it as another step towards deeper denial. Next she'd transfer the guilt to me, criticising me for excessive boozing. I could see it coming.

'You sure?' she persisted.

'Yeah, I've got to drive. And I'm afraid I can't stay long. What did you want to see me about?'

'Sandy is on her way over. I think she should be in on this.'

'In on what?'

Her eyes darted nervously to the clock on the mantelpiece. 'If Sandy left when I phoned, she should be here any minute. Chelmsford's how long from here?'

'Depends on the traffic,' I said. What time d'you phone her?'

'Just before I phoned you.'

'It's just coming up to rush hour. She might do it in forty-five minutes.'

'Are you sure you don't want anything to drink, Freddie?'

I felt anger swelling in my throat. 'If you want a bloody drink, have one. You don't have to keep on about it.'

'There's no need to be like that. Especially as I'm so upset.'

'Mum! Will you just get on with it and tell me what's happened.'

She nodded to the suitcase. 'I knew you was busy yesterday, Freddie, cos Michelle told me you had an important do at this club of yours.'

'What's that got to do with anything?'

With a sudden gust of impatience, she smacked her hand on the table. 'I was coming to that.' She shook her head with frustration. 'You interrupted me... I've lost me thread now.'

I tried to keep calm and spoke softly. 'Mum, Michelle told you I was busy at the club yesterday. So you must have wanted me for something. What was it you wanted?'

Her eyes widened as if startled by the memory. 'Oh yes!' She jerked a thumb at the ceiling. 'The tank in the loft. Problem with the water. Something to do with the ballcock jamming. Anyway, I knew you was busy, so I got Mr Khan's son to have a look at it for me – lives next door but one. And while he was up there, he brought this old suitcase down for me. I had it when I was evacuated. After your father died I wanted to brush all the memories to one side. Too painful they was, so I got all these old keepsakes, put them in the suitcase, and shoved them up in the loft.'

A long pause as she travelled back over the years. Then, finding the silence stifling, she rose unsteadily. 'Well, seeing as you're becoming a bloody misery, son, I'm going to have one. You're welcome to join me if you want.'

I sighed. 'OK, Mum. If you can't beat them, as they say.'

She giggled as she went to the kitchen, her slippers shuffling on the flagstones. 'That's the spirit, Freddie! That's the spirit. Get it?'

She opened the fridge, got a bottle of gin and some tonic, then fetched two tumblers from the sideboard and poured us two large measures. She tipped a small amount of tonic in hers and I had a liberal amount in my glass.

She sniggered as she watched me pour. 'Have some tonic with your gin.'

I ignored it and glanced at my watch. 'I don't want to be late back, Mum. Can't you tell me what it is before Sandy gets here, then…'

I was interrupted by the sound of a key in the front door, followed by Sandy's voice calling out, 'I'm here, Mum!'

As soon as she stepped into the back room I could see the worry showing on my sister's face. Although she had almost reached a milestone birthday – sixty in four months' time – because she was slightly plump, her round face pushed out the wrinkles, giving her skin a lovely smoothness, and her dyed and layered blonde hair added a sort of buxom glamour to her appearance. But now her face was pale and puffy, and her eyes seemed dark and wary, bracing herself for whatever bad news Mum had to disclose. As our eyes met for an instant, we communicated almost telepathically, both suspecting cancer.

The moment had been fleeting and strangers wouldn't have registered our shared concern. Then Sandy suddenly became animated, hurried over to Mum, saying, 'Oh, the poxy traffic – doesn't get any easier,' smothered her with loud kisses, hugged and kissed me, then stood arms akimbo looking down on us as we sipped our drinks.

'Boozing again! I don't know!'

'It's all Freddie's fault. He insisted we had something strong to brace ourselves for what I'm about to tell you.'

I wanted to contradict her but kept it tightly buttoned.

'What is it, Mum?' Sandy said.

'D'you want a drink, Sandy?'

Sandy stared pointedly at me. 'No, some of us have got to drive.'

'Well sit down. You make the place look untidy.'

Sandy sat in the chair next to me, opposite Mum, who took another swallow of gin, fortifying herself for what she was about to reveal.

'For all these years, especially recently, I've had a lot on my mind about your father. But earlier today I got some good and bad news, because at least I've got some answers as to why he did it. Proof.'

I could feel prickles rising from the bottom of my spine to the back of my neck. So this was nothing to do with Mum having a terminal illness. It was to do with that bastard Lennox.

She waited for one of us to cue her, indulging in her moment of drama.

'You mean why he killed himself?' I said.

'He was murdered. Your father was murdered.'

'Oh, come on, Mum,' Sandy said. 'There was an investigation at the time. I know I was only fifteen, but I distinctly remember the coroner's report gave a verdict of...'

Mum raised a hand to silence her. 'Suicide. I know. But if you were being blackmailed by that bastard Mark Lennox... he murdered your father. Killed him. And there's your proof.'

She lifted a photo album on top of the bundle of mementoes in the suitcase, and took a piece of paper from beneath it. The paper was pale blue, A5 size, the sort that comes out of one of those Basildon Bond writing pads. I noticed the triumphant glint in her eyes as she slid the paper across the table. I felt Sandy holding her breath as we read the brief note, which was handwritten and badly spelt.

'You never showed up today. You got till tommorow to make good the damige. I never give you permision to end our arangment. Meet me same time same place with the usual or you know what will happen. Lennox.'

I stared at Mum, waiting for her to say something, but she just stared back at me as if to say I told you so. Sandy was the first to break the silence.

'I never really believed Mark Lennox was blackmailing Dad. I mean, what on earth could Dad have done for him to be blackmailed?'

'Well, there's your proof,' Mum said. 'The note proves it. Not only that, when you was a youngster, Freddie, you saw Lennox meeting up with your Dad that time. And there's this an' all.'

Mum rummaged in the suitcase and threw an envelope on to the table. The envelope was pale blue, matching the notepaper, and I imagined Mark Lennox purchasing them somewhere like W.H. Smith's, probably the first stationery kit the young thug had ever bought, and I imagined him struggling to find the appropriate words without making it obvious it was a blackmailing letter.

The envelope was addressed to Mr Charles Weston at this address, and had been posted with a nine-penny stamp commemorating votes for women. It was franked, and I picked up the envelope and tilted it sideways to see if I could make out the date.

Suddenly I knew why there was a magnifying glass on the table as Mum pushed it towards me. 'The letter was posted two days before your father killed himself. It would have arrived the day before. That bastard Mark Lennox was responsible for your father's death. This letter must have tipped him over the edge.'

I picked up the magnifying glass and held it close to the stamp. I could feel Sandy breathing close to me as she shared the same view of the date. Sure enough, Mum was right – the date was two days before my father committed suicide.

I slammed the magnifying glass down, my temper rising. 'You're right, Mum. This is all the proof I need that Lennox had it in for Dad.'

Sandy put a hand on my arm. 'Hang on, Freddie. Dad had a steady job. We were never really that well off. Comfortable – we didn't really want for anything. So what on earth could Lennox have blackmailed him about? Dad was honest, I'm sure of it. And there's nothing in this letter that tells us he was being blackmailed.'

'Oh, come on, Sandy,' I protested. 'Dad put in a lot of overtime at the docks. He earned decent money back then.'

'He'd been saving,' Mum chipped in. 'A nest egg for the future and his kids' education. But when they checked his savings account after he'd gone, there was no money in it. Not a farthing. It was all gone. That bastard Lennox must've took it all.'

Sandy shook her head and I noticed the fearful quiver in her voice as she spoke.

'I still don't see what Dad could have been blackmailed about. Maybe he spent the money gambling and lost it all.'

I picked up the envelope and waved it in front of Sandy. 'This is the proof that Lennox was responsible for Dad's death. What more do you want? The letter contains a threat, and the fact that it was delivered the day before Dad topped himself shows he was desperate. Perhaps he did do something dodgy for Lennox and later regretted it and didn't want to get involved again, but Lennox wouldn't let him off the hook. Whatever it was, it's all here in the letter. And Lennox is one hundred per cent responsible.'

'So what are you going to do about it? Cause more trouble and heartache. If you get involved, Freddie, and try to get Lennox back for what he did, you'll put your own family in danger. Is that what you want?'

'She's right, son,' Mum said. 'Don't get involved.'

Sandy suddenly snapped at her, 'Then why the hell did you have to show us this fucking letter? Eh? You knew what it would do to, Freddie. You know what he's like. Couldn't you have burnt it? Got rid of it?'

'Please,' I pleaded with Sandy, 'don't blame Mum. Think what it must have been like for her, finding Dad that day. And then having to live with the nightmare, the memory of the way she found him.'

It was during the school holidays that it happened, and I was with Sandy down by the sea at Greatstone, where Mum's sister, Aunty Viv had a flat. We spent most of the summer down there while Mum and Dad worked, until that fateful day when Mum arrived home from her auxiliary nursing job to find Dad hanging from the stairwell. I tried to imagine what it must have been like for her, which is why I always made allowances for her boozing.

Her eyes glassy, Mum looked down shamefully into her gin and mumbled, 'I'm sorry. I just thought you ought to know. I thought… I thought it would help us all to understand why your father did it. Instead of leaving us wondering…'

Exhausted by emotion, Mum's voice weakened into a silent longing, like a whispered prayer.

Sandy turned and looked me in the eye. 'So tell me, Freddie, what *are* you going to do now you know?'

I realised my jaw was clamped tight and my hands were balled into fists. The awful, sudden silence was oppressive as I tried to find my voice. I looked into Sandy's eyes, penetrating in their fear and desperation, and I felt nothing but a numb stupidity. I wanted to reassure her. Say something to calm the pent up atmosphere which had hit the top of the temperature gauge.

'Well?' she demanded, her lips stretched tight, thinning into a hard expression of confrontation.

A small petulant shrug was all I gave her, but it was enough to provoke a forceful slam of her hand bang on the table top. Mum, I noticed, automatically grabbed her gin glass in case it got knocked over with Sandy's temper tantrum.

'No need for that sulky expression,' big sister squawked, glaring at me, eyes fired with passion. 'I know you only too well, Freddie. I know what you're capable of. I know some of the things you got up to when you was a mercenary. I heard stories.'

A hot and cold surge of alarm in my body as my brain registered the shock. What the hell had Sandy heard about my exploits? I thought that part of my past was well and truly buried. Did she know about the boy soldiers? It was one of the most shameful experiences of my life and not one I wanted anyone I loved to know anything about.

'What are you talking about?' I said, my voice subdued and dry. 'What have you heard about me?'

I gulped some gin and tonic but it didn't quench my sudden thirst.

'I heard stories on the grapevine about you and some of your mercenary pals.'

'Where was this?' I said. 'Out in Africa or the Middle East?'

'London. Apparently you had a row in a pub in Swiss Cottage and bit off someone's thumb.'

I laughed with relief, glad it had nothing to do with the shameful Angolan episode.

'That's not funny, Freddie. It's disgusting.'

She shivered hugely, like she'd just been for an ice cold swim.

'Look, Sandy, let me explain.' Calmer now. Relief in my voice. 'That's called Chinese whispers. I was out with a few pals of mine, and we had our girlfriends with us, but the thumb incident had nothing to do with me. It was my mate Bill. This geezer – total stranger – barged into his girl and she spilt her drink. So Bill confronted the bloke. Asked him to apologise. But the geezer wouldn't. Said he never would apologise to a woman, cos they were all slags. Bill gave him another warning, told him again to apologise to her. But he wouldn't. Instead, he offered Bill his hand, saying he would shake on all us men sticking together. That's when Bill grabbed his hand and bit off his thumb off at the joint.'

Sandy pulled a grotesque expression. 'That's disgusting. Bit it right off?'

'Well, it was hanging on by a thread. The guy was in shock. It took a moment for it to register. Then when he realised what had happened, saw his thumb dangling by a thin piece of skin, he ran off into the night. Christ knows what became of him.'

Her fears dispelled, Sandy blew her cheeks out noisily. 'And all these years I thought that was you who done that.'

I smiled with relief, truthfully glad I wasn't the culprit on that particular occasion, and was even more relieved she knew nothing about Angola.

'Wish you could bite *that* bastard's thumb off,' Mum said, a small nod at the letter. 'It would serve him right.'

We knew she meant Lennox, and there was no escaping the fact that Mum wanted the bastard to pay for what he had done. In spite of not wanting me to put my own life in danger.

Sandy frowned deeply, turned to look at me with begging eyes as she placed a hand over mine.

'Freddie, now you know Lennox was responsible for Dad's death, I hope to God for you and Michelle's sake you're not planning on—'

'Look, Sandy,' I interrupted, 'I still don't know why Dad killed himself, and what Lennox had on him. And there's only one person who can tell me and that's Lennox himself.'

'Oh, and he's bound to share that ancient history with you,' she replied. 'You think he's going to tell you after all these years? "Yes, I was blackmailing your father and here's the reason why." Forget it, Freddie. Just forget it.' She looked across at Mum. 'You too, Mrs Gordon's Gin.'

Said in an attempt to lighten the situation.

'I suspect you're right, Sandy,' I said. 'Maybe it's best we just forget about it. And I'm off to Spain on Thursday, so I want to forget it and enjoy some golf.'

'I think that's best, Freddie. Dragging up the past like this can only hurt people both now and in the future. I've heard about Lennox and his dirty little organisation, if anyone deserves to be called evil, it's him. And he controls a lot of loathsome bastards too.'

Mum knocked back the last of her drink, examined the empty glass wishing the gin fairy would wave her magic wand, and said, 'Shame they couldn't have put him away years ago, like they did the Krays. We might have had some sort of justice then.'

'Not really,' I said. 'A nice cosy cell in his twilight years and enough money to pay for some of life's luxuries.'

Sandy's brittle tone returned. 'So what do you suggest? Taking the law into your own hands?'

'No. Freddie's right,' Mum said. 'If they ever put him away, he'll have a nice colour TV and all mod cons. It ain't right.'

'So what do you suggest, Mum?' Sandy's voice became shrill. 'Send Freddie after him with some of his ex-army pals?'

Not a bad idea, I thought. Go mob handed.

'And then where does it end? Lennox's gang comes after Freddie – and even worse, his family. Why don't we just let it go? It's been well over forty years for Christ's sake.'

I decided it was time to cool the situation, let everyone think I was going to back down and forget Lennox killed my old man.

'Yeah, you're right as usual, Sis,' I said, and pecked her cheek reassuringly. 'I'll forget any thoughts about getting the truth out of Lennox. I promise. The idea's ridiculous. There's no point in pursuing it. Time to let it go.'

Mum sniffed loudly. 'That's it, Freddie. You go off to Spain, have a good time and forget all about your father hanging his self.'

I was about to reassure her, tell her I might find someone else to sort Lennox out – tell her anything she wanted to hear – but Sandy leapt in first.

'Why do you do it, Mum? What's wrong with you?'

Mum's eyes widened in girlish innocence. 'Do what, sweetheart?'

'Don't pretend you don't know what I'm talking about. You know bloody well how Freddie's bottled it up over the years, so that it's become an obsession. So stop winding him up now he's agreed to let it drop.'

Like fuck I had.

'And you making him feel guilty is unfair. Totally unfair! It's not Freddie's fault if Dad hanged himself. Freddie was a youngster and it had nothing to do with him. If anything, it was Dad's fault for not facing up to whatever hold Lennox had on him.'

I gritted my teeth, knowing this was not what Sandy should be telling Mum. Bad enough Dad committed suicide, but at least if Mum could hang on to the notion that Lennox was responsible, and Dad succumbed to the pressure from the gangster leaning on him, giving the balance of his mind a nasty wrench.

As if she sensed she might have gone too far, Sandy leant forwards and held Mum's hand, speaking quietly. 'Mum, I'm sorry, I didn't mean to blame Dad. But whatever the reason, maybe he panicked. We all do rash things from time to time – things which we might later regret – but it's over now, and nothing we say or do is going to bring him back or make things right after all these years.'

I noticed tears glistening in Mum's eyes as she fought to control them. She wiped one eye hastily with the back of two fingers and nodded as she said, 'I know you're right, Sandy love, it's just I've looked for answers all these years, and now part of it's come to me. It might have been better if I hadn't found this letter. But now that I have…'

Sudden silence. Sandy and I watched Mum staring at the letter as if it was a venomous snake about to strike. I thought for a minute she might freak out and tear it to shreds. But she just sat immobilised, eyes fixed on the offending note. I felt deeply sorry for her, and almost wished she'd never found the damned letter.

All these years we suspected – no, we bloody well knew – that Lennox was responsible, and the evidence had been sitting there in that battered old suitcase in Mum's loft waiting to be discovered. But now we had the proof, what good would it do? I was stymied. There was no way I could get to Lennox, who was well protected by his mob. And even if I could get to him, it was highly unlikely I could get him to spill his guts. The truth was a half-truth, frustratingly incomplete, as we were left wondering what the root cause of Dad's suicide was.

But it was Mum I felt most sorry for. As her short term memory got poorer, the long term one improved, and the past now plagued her with unanswered questions, which for most of the years following Dad's death she had managed to shove into a safe compartment somewhere. But now Lennox's note had reopened the file and the torment had started all over again, as if Dad's suicide had happened only yesterday. I felt the suppressed anger hurting in my chest, aware that not only was Lennox responsible for Dad's death, he was now tormenting – if not killing – my mother. And as I watched the effect this was having on her, I vowed that Lennox was going to pay the price for what he did to our family. I knew it would be risky, but if I didn't go for payback then I would regret it for the rest of my life. Maybe Sandy and Michelle were right. Maybe I was obsessed with vengeance and the need to seek retribution for our family.

As if Sandy could feel the vibes of hatred welling up inside me, she put a steadying hand on my arm and squeezed.

'Let's just hope,' she said, 'Lennox gets his comeuppance. I truly believe that what goes around comes around.'

Which is what Mal MacIntyre had told me. And I thought it was a lot of bollocks then. No, the only way it would come around for Lennox was if I did something about it. But I had to set Sandy's mind at rest. Make her think I'd accepted the defeat, and was willing to let God and the afterlife punish Lennox. I sighed pointedly and stood up.

'I think you're probably right, Sis,' I said. 'Lennox has so many enemies, and one way or another one of them will get to him. Especially as he's older. He'll be more vulnerable. Now I'd better shoot off, otherwise Michelle'll wonder what's up.'

But I knew it was far from over. Lennox was an evil scumbag and it was time he paid the price for what he'd done, not only to my father, but for all the other poor bastards he'd terrified, mutilated and murdered during a long history of villainy.

But first I had to come up with a decent plan of action, and I hadn't a clue where to start.

14
EL SID

Just before we arrived at the drop off point at Stansted airport, Michelle asked me why I was really going to Spain, as if she was trying to surprise me into inadvertently blurting out some half-lie. She was definitely suspicious, mainly I think because I had decided to leave my clubs at home, telling her my pal Sid had bought himself a new set and I could use his old ones, which saved me having to wait for them at the carousel, and I could now travel with hand luggage only. I was worried in case she thought I might be going to Marbella to indulge in some extramarital, so I promised her faithfully that apart from the few rounds of golf, Sid might have a business opportunity to put my way and swore I would tell her everything on my return. She seemed satisfied, although I could tell there was still a niggling doubt bubbling away inside her, and all because I wasn't taking my clubs. But there was no point. For the first time in years, my visit to Sid would not involve golf. We had other plans.

During the flight, I attempted to concentrate on a John Grisham novel I bought at the bookstall before leaving, but my mind kept wandering back to Mark Lennox and the note. I'd known all along he had some sort of hold over my father, but now I was determined to find out exactly what that was. I tried pushing it to the back of my mind, determined to enjoy this trip to Marbella, but Lennox's ugly mug kept intruding, and my mind alternated between scheming on how I could wring the truth out of him and how I could have some lucrative fun at the expense of this tabloid hack, someone who I felt deserved everything she had coming to her. Because of what she did for a living and the way she thought she was conning me, I was never going to lose any sleep over this caper. Sid might, of course, but only in the most pleasurable way, as long as he didn't mind copulating with a scheming bitch who was only after an exclusive double-page spread. But I was sure he could manage – for Queen and country and all that!

When the plane touched down at Malaga and I stepped out into early afternoon glare at the top of the landing steps, it was like stepping into a furnace and I was almost glad to have elbowed the golf. Sitting in the shade sipping ice cold beer was all I craved from this trip.

I made my way quickly through customs, checked the arrival board for Ali's scheduled flight – which I was pleased to note was on time – and made my way to the concourse outside to check the times of the buses leaving for Marbella. There was one due not long after her arrival, so there was no sense in forking out for a taxi. I had about an hour to kill, so I went into the nearby bar and got myself an ice cold bottle of San Miguel.

As I sat thoughtfully sipping my drink, I watched a thin-faced man of about seventy, face like parchment, shuffling to the drinks cabinet to get a small bottle of white wine, and I suddenly became aware of my tension, the way my jaw was tightly clenched. The man bore a vague resemblance to Mark Lennox, and I told myself not to be so stupid. It was irrational. When I observed the man closely, the gentle and polite smile he gave the assistant serving him, I realised he was nothing like the gangster. It was me becoming uptight again.

The next hour crawled by as I tried to free my mind from dwelling on Lennox. Instead, my mind replayed the scene in the Liquid Velvet with Crystal and his cronies and I cheered up considerably as I thought about it, even though the cost of the evening still left a sour taste in my mouth. But I thought I might be able to recoup those losses if everything went as planned.

★

Ali arrived looking sexier than I remembered her from our dinner date, and I almost felt cheated that it was Sid and not me she'd be making a play for. But then I reminded myself about what she really did for a living and told myself she was a lying, cheating bitch and Sid was welcome to anything she offered. I know I was also lying and cheating, but I felt justified and I had no qualms about what I was doing.

We found a seat near the back of the coach, far from any other passengers, where we could talk without being overheard. Ali gave me a tentative smile, and I became aware of her reserve, her reluctance to throw too many questions at me and arouse my suspicion.

'We'll get a cab from the bus station to my mate's house,' I said.

'And does this mate of yours have a name, or will he be using an alias?' She giggled to show this was all a game and she was a simple girl from the sticks enjoying a big adventure.

'Sid's his real name. Sid Finch.'

'And he doesn't mind me – a stranger – knowing his real name?'

I shrugged. 'He doesn't give a monkey's. The police haven't got anything on him. They've got their suspicions, naturally, but no proof at all. Most people know him down here as Sid – they even jokingly refer to him as El Sid on the Costa del Crime.'

'I can't wait to meet him.' She lowered her voice and shifted closer to me. 'How much did you say he got of that fifty-three million?'

'Only four to five.'

'So what happened to the rest of it?'

'Police recovered some of it. Not much. Some of the other gang members got more than Sid.'

'Even though he masterminded it.'

'Sid's not greedy. He just knew he had to get away quickly because the rest of the gang were a bunch of idiots. And he set himself up with a little bar, a nice house – nothing too lavish to draw attention to himself. I mean, there were rumours about him organising the Tonbridge job, but no one could prove a thing. That's why he didn't mind me bringing you out to meet him. I told him…'

I deliberately let my sentence trail off, leading her to prompt me.

'You told him what?'

'That you're a gangster groupie.'

I tried to read her expression but it was hard to interpret, although there did seem to be a glimmer of amusement in her eyes.

'I'm sorry,' I added. 'But what am I supposed to think? You've made a special trip out to Spain to meet a successful criminal, knowing full well he's a philandering dog. So I naturally assumed you get turned on by geezers who live outside the law.'

She laughed, easing the sudden tension between us, and shook her head. 'No way am I a gangster groupie – or didn't they call them molls years ago?'

'So why the fascination with my mate Sid?'

'To be honest, I don't really know. But I've given it considerable thought and I suppose it's because I'm in a dull job and most of the men I've been out with are real semi-detached, safe, suburban types. Just for once I'd like to meet someone with a bit of danger attached to them. Someone who takes risks.'

'Well, I hope you're not going to be too disappointed when you meet Sid. He may have pulled off one of the world's biggest robberies, but he's now leading a pretty safe life down here.'

'Yes, but I expect he's got some fascinating stories to tell.'

I had to look away at that point. I didn't want to give her the smallest glimpse of what was going on in my head. I've got you sussed, sweetheart, I am thinking. And you'll do anything to get your grubby little story.

I stared out of the bus window as we flashed along the motorway, passing blocks of bright yellow apartments scattered across the hillside. The sunshine and sea view leant them a glamour they didn't deserve. If you dumped a similar block in Plaistow or Canning Town, it would be just another grotty high-rise.

As if Ali had said the wrong thing, sensing she might have let slip an ulterior motive for making this trip, she asked me what was wrong.

I looked her in the eyes and told her Sid had never been in trouble with the law, and planned and executed the Tonbridge job – his only job – and I wouldn't want to see my mate stitched up for it if she gossiped to the wrong person back in England.

Her eyes dripped with Hughie Green-type sincerity as she took my hand and assured me his secret was safe with her.

I'll bet it is, I thought.

★

We caught a cab from the bus station, which took us to the outskirts of Marbella, up into the hills, where Sid's house was. His house was more impressive than his bar, which was really a bit of a dive, but it gave him a modest living. I had persuaded Sid to take time off from work because if Ali were to visit his bar it might start her wondering why a multi-millionaire would invest money in such an unexceptional watering-hole. His house, though, was reasonably impressive. Sid had won five numbers and a bonus ball on the lottery, rewarding him with a little under two-hundred K, and he heard on the gangster grapevine about a villain who had to scarper pretty sharpish and wanted to offload his gaff quickly to a cash buyer. Sid also had a mini-cab business in Romford and, when he won the lottery, he sold the business and moved to Spain, with enough cash to buy himself the large house with a pool and the small bar which would provide him with an income, without having to graft as hard as he had running the cab firm in Romford. And the great thing about our little scam was the fact that Sid's fortunes changed in May 2006, just months after the Tonbridge robbery. So if Ali checked him out, as I was sure she would, she would discover he sold his business quickly and headed for Spain not long after the heist.

As the taxi stopped outside two wrought iron gates barring entrance to my mate's house, I asked the driver to press the horn. He gave it three long blasts and in a moment the gates swung open and we were driven into a sloped and circular driveway in front of Sid's imposing house. A furtive sideways glance was enough to tell me that so far Ali was reasonably impressed.

I paid the driver and, instead of turning in the ample space of the driveway, he reversed out onto the quiet road. Sid appeared on the balcony at the front of the house, smiling with his hands spread wide in a welcoming gesture. We walked up the steps to meet him beneath the roofed lounging area (loggia I think it's called) with its curved arches, past the tiered and sloping gardens to the left of the house and level patio and good sized swimming pool to the right.

'Hey, Freddie!' he called. 'Welcome, my old mate.'

I gave Sid a hug, then stepped back to introduce him to Ali. I could see them assessing one another, seeing if they were tolerably attracted to each other, both knowing what the score was without knowing the real reasons and motive for her visit. And what was so great was that she didn't know that we knew why she was there. Never had the proverb set a thief to catch a thief been so apt, and it gave me a buzz thinking about it.

I could see by the way Ali looked at him, like a machine electronically scanning his features, that she found him reasonably attractive. OK, so Sid is no oil painting and has a weak chin and a bulbous nose; but these defects apart, his is a pleasant face with a mouth that turns upwards, and slightly rugged features hinting at a man who enjoys life to the full, and his large blue eyes contain a Mediterranean sparkle and a look of good-humoured expectation, as if waiting to laugh at the punchline in a joke. And his jet black hair, worn long but not excessively so, has only the tiniest flecks of grey coming through. But then he's ten years younger than me.

Once the introductions were out of the way, Sid offered us a drink, but Ali asked if she could freshen up first. Sid showed her to her room, with its en-suite bathroom, and returned alone with two bottles of San Miguel which he'd fetched from the kitchen.

I sat by the table, grinned at him and we clinked bottles. 'Good to see you, mate,' he said. 'And nice of you to bring me a little present this time.'

I chuckled suggestively before replying, 'Those spiders eat their mates once they've had sex. Watch yourself.'

'But this time the male gets to eat the female. Metaphorically speaking, of course.'

I raised my bottle. 'I'll drink to that!' And took a long swig of ice cold lager. I caught myself looking furtively over my shoulder, and dropped my voice. 'You read that book I suggested?'

'Three times. I know the details of the robbery backwards. Names, places, everything.'

The book was *Heist* by Howard Sounes, all about the Tonbridge robbery, and I had read it a couple of years ago. When I came up with the idea of this wind-up — because that's all it was to begin with — I phoned Sid and asked him to buy a copy. I don't think he took it seriously at first, but when I came up with the idea of using the wind-up to con the tabloid, Sid began to take his research and homework seriously.

'Well done, Sid. You know she'll check the facts once she gets back.'

'Sure, but I can remember most of the relevant stuff. And the few details I miss — well, we are talking about something that happened over six years ago, so the details might be a little fuzzy after all the sex, sea, and sangria.'

'Incidentally, what have you done with the book? I hope you haven't left it lying around.'

'Credit me with some sense. It's under lock and key at the bar. So it's there if I need to check up on anything. Incidentally, did you ever find out which rag she works for?'

'*Sunday Express.*' I looked at my watch. 'Soon as we've had a bit of three way chat — so as not to make her suspicious by leaving too sudden — I'll slope off to Estepona to see Mal MacIntyre. He and his missus have just bought a place there. I think they've got two bedrooms, so I might stay the night and it'll give you and her some breathing space.'

Sid smirked like a naughty schoolboy. 'This is like one of those spy scenarios with a honeytrap.'

'How come?'

'Because it's always afterwards the geezer gives away the secrets. The pillow talk when he's most relaxed and off his guard.'

'So you'll be saving your best confession for the pillow talk tomorrow morning?'

'Yeah, of course. Just a few appetizers over dinner, showing how reluctant I am to open up completely. But when tomorrow comes I'll be putty in her hands.'

We talked for a while about old times, people we had known, and kept off the subject of the scam. When Ali returned half an hour later, looking extremely attractive in a tight tank-top and mini-skirt, we indulged in small talk and which villains we knew who were currently in residence on the Costa del Crime, giving her a few juicy stories to whet her appetite. She seemed surprised when I told her I wouldn't be joining the two of them for dinner, but I hinted that there was a bit of skulduggery going on with the chap I was visiting, and I would see them both around lunchtime the next day.

Ali nodded, accepting the arrangements, then took her mobile out of her handbag and said to Sid, 'Great place you have here. Mind if I grab a quick snap, maybe from the bottom of the steps, looking up at the house, maybe with you on the top step looking down proudly at your estate. Just a souvenir. One for the album and memory lane.'

'Sure,' Sid said, and took up what he thought might look like a successful villain pose, leaning against the pillar nonchalantly, hands in pockets. I lay back out of sight in the reclining chair, and as Sid glanced at me just before adopting his pose, I gave him a smile and a wink.

It was working.

★

It was quite a drinking session we had at Mal's apartment, and his wife, Janice, was no slouch when it came to knocking back the brandy and Coke. Mal's face was now a deep purple hue; he perspired terribly and coughed incessantly as he inhaled killer smoke into his lungs, giving me good reason to limit my own intake, much as I would have liked to indulge my own habit every time I watched him light up. We eventually got to bed around three or four – I don't really remember – and slept until ten. I couldn't hear a peep from Mal and Janice's room, so I threw on a bathrobe I found hanging in the wardrobe, made myself coffee, and sat out on the northern-facing balcony, thankfully out of the sun's glare. As I lay in a reclining chair thinking about Sid and his devious lover, I wondered if she was lapping up his tale of robbery. I almost felt pangs of jealousy, guessing how he must be enjoying himself, both in deception and physical pleasure.

I could picture the scene.

★

They had made love twice in the night and, in between the first and second time, Sid had given her the opening she needed, by saying her love-making was exciting, but in a different way to the adrenaline which raced through his body during and immediately after the robbery. She lay in the half dark, her head close to his on the pillow, her breathing light and controlled, and he fancied he could hear the cogs turning in her head as she cautiously slipped him her first question.

'So you didn't participate in the actual robbery?'

'That's right. I was like a film director. My name's on the credits, but you won't catch sight of me in the film.'

'I thought that chap who's in jail in Morocco was the leader.'

He knew she was testing him without mentioning the robber Lee Murray by name, which would be a dead giveaway.

'The robbery was my idea and I planned it down to the last detail. I knew some of them would get caught, cos they were a bunch of tossers, so I arranged for most of the money cages to go to the farm in Detling, where I knew I could grab a few million and get away pretty sharpish, leaving no trail at all.'

'But if they were that incompetent, how come they pulled off the biggest robbery ever?'

'Oh, they got away with a massive haul all right, but most of them are behind bars. If they'd done everything like I said, that might not have happened. They might have got clean away.'

'So when did you first get the idea to rob that building? I think most people said they had no idea it contained so much money. It was just… well… just an insignificant looking building.'

'You might find this hard to believe but I was visiting a mate in Tonbridge, and we overheard a conversation in a local pub – someone running down this employment agency because they didn't thoroughly vet the staff they sent to Medway House where all this money was stored. That set me thinking: if I could get someone employed there – an inside man – we might find a way to rob it. Of course, I was only half serious at first. I never thought it would amount to anything. Until I met this Albanian geezer in a pub in Tunbridge Wells. Weird name he had till you knew how to pronounce it. Ermir – and let me see if I can still remember how he spelt his surname – I think it was H-Y-S-E-N-A-J. Pronounced Hoosenay. Nothing like how it looked.'

A detail like this would give his tale credibility and Sid felt a glow of pride at having memorised what might appear to be trivial, but what might prove to be vitally important if he was going to convince her he was telling the truth.

She stirred beside him, moved closer and kissed him on the lips, her hands caressing his chest and he felt the velvety smoothness of her tongue. They became more intense as she took hold of his already erect penis and began making love again. Just before he entered her, it briefly crossed his mind that perhaps her investigative journalism was a stimulus and the deception turned her on. As he buried his lips in her neck, arched backwards, then thrust himself forcefully inside her, he smiled, not just from the sheer pleasure of the act itself, but from his own deception and the fact that she thought it was the other way round.

After a much longer session of lovemaking, their bodies thrusting like opponents in a contest, they eventually climaxed before falling into an exhausted back-to-back sleep, neither of them wanting to pretend they had indulged in anything more than an enjoyable leisure activity.

They woke early, just after six, and made love once more. Afterwards, as Sid lay back, giving her an appreciative smile, he knew this was confession time, when he really had to pretend that she was someone who was special and someone with whom he could safely tell his darkest secrets to. But he knew that to begin speaking about the robbery would arouse her suspicion, and waited for her to prompt him, although he also knew she was unable to speak too knowledgbly about the robbery, so as not to arouse *his* suspicion.

As she lay next to him, leaning slightly raised on one elbow, she gave him a gentle smile and said, 'Was my lovemaking as exciting as that robbery?'

Good one, he thought. Nice lead in.

He chuckled roguishly. 'It was fantastic, sweetheart. But the thing about robbery is that it gives you a buzz unlike any other. See, it's not just about money and the things money can buy.'

'So what is it about?'

'It's about the planning and then going into action. Taking a big risk and getting away with it.'

'I still don't understand how you got away with it and the others got caught.'

He grinned and tapped the side of his nose. And then he launched into his confession, telling her everything he knew, a cockcrow strutting confession in which he bragged about the way he had directed the operation, not only fooling the police but the other robbers as well, boasting about the ideas he had passed on to Lee Murray, a thick cage fighter who couldn't possibly organise a sting like the multi-million pound robbery which he, Sid, had masterminded. He gave her names, dates, and countless details which Freddie and he had discussed as clinchers to make the story sound authentic.

Once the story ended, Sid offered her coffee, and she said she was gasping for a cup. He went out to the kitchen and moments later he thought he heard her getting out of bed, so he tiptoed to the kitchen door and listened. He could have sworn he heard her voice, maybe speaking to someone on her mobile. Just a couple of words which he couldn't catch and then silence. Presumably she had cut the brief call.

As he waited for the kettle to boil, and spooned instant coffee into mugs, he heard her mobile ringing. He tiptoed back to the kitchen door and listened intently. She spoke louder this time, clearly for his benefit, and he heard her saying, 'Oh Mum! That's terrible. How is he?' A pause and then she said, 'I'll come home right away. The next available flight. No! I must. I'll be home just as soon as I can. Bye, Mum. And try not to worry. I'm sure he'll be OK.'

She ended the call, and Sid hurriedly crossed the room to finish making the coffee. He smiled to himself and muttered, 'You bitch.'

★

It was almost noon and still Mal and Janice hadn't surfaced, but then we'd all had a skinful the previous night. But Mal's boozing was now out of control, and that went for his missus as well, and I wondered which one of them would be the first to snuff it. Mind you, I'd given it a fair old hammering as well, so I promised myself I would take it easy for today.

I had shoved my mobile into the pocket of the bathrobe, and thought I might give Michelle a quick ring. Olivia had a rehearsal for another show next week, Jackie had offered to record and operate the sound for it, and I felt it was my duty to ring and show parental interest. I was just about to dial when it vibrated in my hand, and the screen gave Michelle's name.

I felt annoyed she was ringing, because I wanted to be the instigator of the call, the person who kept in touch, showing how thoughtful and caring I was. Now she would think I hadn't given them a second thought, which was untrue.

I pressed the mobile's receive button and injected enthusiasm into my voice. 'Michelle! Sweetheart! You're not gonna believe this. I was just this very minute about to ring you. Phone was in my hand ready to make the call. I want to know how Jackie and Olivia are shaping up for the big rehearsal tonight and…'

Her voice cut in, sharp as a razor, 'Freddie, listen to me. You've got to drop everything and come home.'

'What?'

'The police want to speak to you. You're in big trouble, you idiot.'

'Why? What's going on?'

She began shouting, her voice vibrating in my ear, 'You stupid, stupid idiot. I asked you to get rid of that bouncer from the Kismet Club. And now it's too late. Your fucking business will be ruined over this.'

I felt my stomach heave as she said it. 'What happened?' I mumbled, though I could guess, and my stomach lurched again. And then she hit me with the shit news. Bob Crystal had freaked out again. A quiet Thursday night at the Kismet, and a punter who had given him some stick was now on a life support machine. If the bloke didn't recover, Bob Crystal was looking at a manslaughter charge, and I was being blamed as his employer, because Mark Lennox had told the police that he worked for me.

'I told Mark Lennox he was no longer in my employ,' I yelled back.

'Did you though?'

'Yes, I bloody well did. Lennox had already told me my staff had become his staff since he's taken over the Kismet, and if I didn't like it I could go and fuck myself.'

'Oh, Freddie! What a mess.' She sounded tearful and desperate now. 'If Lennox insists he was employing someone who works for you…'

'He can't do that,' I broke in. 'And the police aren't going to believe a creep like Lennox.'

'Oh, and they're bound to believe every word *you* say.'

'What's that supposed to mean?'

'It means you don't exactly rub shoulders with the cream of society. More like the dregs most of the time.'

'Look,' I began, trying to quell my anger, 'I've never been in trouble with the police.'

'Until now.'

'I'm not in any trouble now,' I yelled, my frustration turning into anger. But emotions are sometimes hard to interpret speaking on a mobile, so my raised voice could just mean a bad signal. 'Once I explain to the police what happened, there's nothing they can do about it. Christ! Anyone would think I was responsible, for fuck's sake. This is Lennox's doing, and you know it is. It's always Lennox. He's like Satan, always lurking in the background, waiting to deliver us to evil.'

I was almost proud of that last statement and waited for Michelle to speak, like I was waiting for a round of applause. When she eventually spoke, her voice was subdued and pleading.

'Please, Freddie, come home as soon as you can. I want you to sort this out.'

'Do the police know I'm in Spain?'

'Yes, I told them you were due back on Monday but…'

'OK, Michelle,' I interrupted. 'I'll be home as soon as I can get an earlier flight. If not tonight – I mean Friday night could be busy – then first flight tomorrow morning. Then I'll speak to the cops first thing on Monday. And I'll sort it. I promise. Try not to worry. It's going to be OK. I promise. Give the girls a big hug for me.'

She mumbled a routine 'I love you' and we hung up.

I stood up and poked my head indoors. I still couldn't hear any indication that Mal and Janice were about to surface, so I showered, dressed, scribbled them a note thanking them for their hospitality, apologised for dashing off, and said I would be in touch.

It was a short walk to the centre of Estepona, from where I picked up a cab and headed for Sid's house. When I arrived I was surprised to find him out on his front balcony, lying in the shade, swigging from a bottle of San Miguel. He offered me a self-satisfied grin, and looked up at me through half-lidded eyes.

I lowered my voice. 'Ali still in bed?'

He shook his head. 'Ah-ah. You don't have to whisper, Freddie. She's gone.'

'Gone?' I yelped. 'What do you mean, she's gone?'

'I mean, our bird has flown. But I did not have to sleep in the bath. Nor did I have to set fire to the house.'

'You're not making any sense, Sid. You pissed already?'

'You know: the Beatles song, "Norwegian Wood." But it doesn't matter. I think everything's gone according to plan. After this morning's shag, I played the part of the gullible villain boasting about his money conquests, and she lapped it up. Then, while I made coffee, I heard her making a call on her mobile. Minutes later someone called back, and she had this over-the-top conversation – clearly for my benefit – pretending it was her mother ringing to say her father'd been rushed to hospital with a heart attack and could she come home right away. You should have seen her face when she stood in the kitchen doorway and told me the bad news. I swear she'd gone a whiter shade of pale. What an actress.'

'What a bitch.'

Sid grinned hugely. 'Yeah, that's what I said when I heard her on the phone. But you know what this means, don't you, Freddie? It means she's fallen for my story and she's rushed back to get it in for this Sunday.'

'Let's hope you're right.'

'I know I'm right, mate. I can feel it in me bones. You wanna drink?'

I shook my head. 'Got any sparkling water in your fridge?'

'Am I hearing things?'

'No, I intend to sober up. Michelle phoned me with some bad news.'

'What's up?'

I went and fetched some mineral water from his fridge, came back, sat down and told him the whole story of Crystal and his wicked uncle, and what had happened at the Kismet Club. Then I launched into the tale about Lennox and the blackmail letter.

'So what are you gonna do about it?' he asked as I finished my story.

'I'm going to book a flight for tomorrow morning – should get one on a Saturday easily enough. I'm going to text Michelle and tell her I couldn't get one tonight. We will then go out and have a decent lunch. Swim in your pool this afternoon. Quick snooze. Then you and me can have a night out on the town.'

'I didn't mean that. I meant what are you gonna do about this Lennox arsehole?'

'I don't know yet. But I've got to do something.'

And it was true. I had to find a way of settling the score and finding out the truth about what went on between Lennox and my father all those years ago. The trouble was, I hadn't a clue how to go about it. I just knew there had to be a way.

I lay back in the reclining chair and tilted the bottled water to take a swig. It gushed out of the neck and doused my polo shirt. 'Shit!' I said, sitting up and wiping the shirt with the flat of my hand.

Sid chuckled. 'It's only water, Freddie. Nothing to be frightened of.'

Click. The old light bulb moment. Just a vague thought to begin with, a sort of mental overview, but then my mind slipped into gear and began to buzz with possibilities. I now had an idea of what I was going to do with Lennox. I just needed to work on the finer points of the plot and call on the assistance of my old mercenary chum, Bill Turner. And this time I felt he would have no hesitation in giving me his support, because he knows how much the reason for my old man's death has bugged me all these years.

15
PAYBACK

I arrived back at Stansted on Saturday afternoon and Michelle came to pick me up. Her reception was a little frosty but I managed to persuade her that I would go to the police HQ between Stratford and Forest Gate and talk to the detective who had phoned her and that seemed to set her mind at rest until we got home. But we still had the rest of Saturday and Sunday to get through and by the time she had rattled on about the Kismet situation for the umpteenth time, I was getting bored and irritated and told her there was nothing we could do about it until I took myself off to meet with the law on Monday. I could tell she still wanted to hammer the subject to death until I came up with the idea of phoning Sean and getting a copy of the CCTV footage of Crystal and his mob at the Velvet on the previous Monday. I explained to her that I intended showing it to the coppers – tell them the truth about Crystal and his nephew and withhold nothing about what had happened, because I hadn't broken the law and had nothing to hide. My suggestion calmed Michelle and, after I'd called Sean, I arranged to go over to his house in Muswell Hill on Sunday morning and pick up the disc. I was glad to get out of the house for a couple of hours, which would also give me an opportunity to pick up a copy of the *Sunday Express*.

And there it was: a double-page spread about Sid, the mastermind of the Tonbridge multi-million pound robbery, with a photograph of him at the top of his steps in front of his Spanish house, along with a couple of other photos of him with some girlfriends in the bar in Marbella which she must have downloaded off his Facebook page, and details of how he had planned the robbery, then disappeared with around four million, having quickly sold his mini-cab firm and scarpered to Spain before the law could catch up with him. There were also photos and details of the original robbery with the other robbers Sid had talked to her about.

It had worked. She had fallen for it one-hundred per cent and so, presumably, had her editor. I laughed and punched the air jubilantly before getting out of the car and consigning the newspaper to a litter bin near a bus stop. It wasn't something I wanted Michelle to know about just yet, not with the Kismet fiasco hanging over me.

On Monday morning I arrived at the police station at 10:30 and was kept waiting for twenty minutes, even though I had telephoned to let them know I was on the way. I was eventually taken to the office of Detective Inspector Kevin Bickerton who introduced me to his colleague, Detective Sergeant Mossop. They both looked like the archetypal aggressive and sympathetic cop. Bickerton was jowly and dishevelled, wearing an aggressive, pugnacious expression, whereas Mossop was clean cut with dark close-cropped hair, intelligent lively eyes, and a trim figure in a well-cut suit. Detectives Chalk and Cheese. But appearances can be deceptive. It was Bickerton who spoke quietly and thoughtfully, listening to what I had to say, and it was Mossop, with his faint Lancashire dialect, who interrupted and snapped at me like a disturbed terrier. But when I began my long tale of suffering and how I was duped into employing Dave Crystal's nephew, they both shut up and let me do all the talking. Naturally I edited the story of my employing Bob Crystal to break the guitarist's fingers, telling them that as soon as I and Sean knew how we had been set up, I moved him hastily to the Kismet, intending to get rid of him as soon as Dave Crystal thought he had taken his revenge on the Liquid Velvet. I could see by the way they exchanged dubious looks they didn't believe my story of the club hoax, so I produced the disc with the CCTV footage. They watched it on a computer screen, and both fell about laughing at the behaviour of Crystal and his gang, and also the performance of some of the extras. By the time the disc had ended, I could swear – or was it my imagination? – they looked at me with a certain amount of admiration. Which was when I told them about the conversation I'd had with Lennox, telling me he'd nicked my staff and I had no say in the matter, even though I'd warned him about employing Bob Crystal. They then told me the Kismet had been shut down by the local authorities, pending a thorough investigation. I asked them about the man Crystal had put in hospital. They both exchanged looks and Mossop shrugged.

'Just some scumbag,' he said, 'with a tattoo down his right arm which reads "I like fucking."'

Noticing the way I registered recognition, Bickerton asked me if I'd known the victim, so I told them I recalled seeing him because of his distinctively tasteless tattoo outside the Kismet a few weeks back, when he was approached by the homeless man and told him to get a fucking life.

DS Mossop sniggered. 'What goes around, eh?'

'Yeah, if you believe that superstitious bollocks,' I said.

The interview seemed to be over and I thought I had come through it unscathed. Bickerton nodded at the computer monitor and asked me if they could keep the CCTV disc – no doubt to entertain their colleagues – and we almost parted on good terms. But they always like to have the last word, because I was halfway out of the door when DI Bickerton said, 'We'll be keeping an eye on you, Weston. If we find you employing bouncers with form, you'll be out of the game for good. Comprende?'

I gave him an ever so humble nod and mumbled that I understood.

★

A couple of weeks into June and the weather was abysmal, the worst summer for years, but it was perfect for what I had in mind. On the Friday night we chose to snatch Lennox, as far as Michelle was concerned I was supposed to be sorting out problems at many of my West End clubs and wouldn't be home until the wee small hours.

Bill caught a Central Line train from Shepherd's Bush and I picked him up outside Liverpool Street station. It was almost 10:30 and I had no trouble finding a single yellow line in a side street just off Bishopsgate. It was a filthy night and we both turned up our coat collars and ran as fast as we could through the driving rain back to Bishopsgate and into the famous Dirty Dicks pub. I bought us two large whiskies, which would be our limit, as we needed to be clear-headed for what we were about to do, but at the same time we needed some Dutch courage.

There were not many customers in the pub because trade drops off in most city pubs early on, and we found a darkened corner in which to sit. As we sat I saw Bill tapping the bulge under his arm.

'Got the weapon?' I asked.

He smiled and his eyes glinted. 'He won't know what's hit him.'

'He's getting on in years. Let's hope it doesn't kill him.'

Bill shrugged and pursed his lips. 'If he's got a dodgy ticker then… but I can't think of another way. Can you?'

I shook my head. 'We'll stick to the plan we've got. Here's to it.' We clinked glasses and sipped our whiskies, both silently anticipating the explosive night that lay ahead.

I looked down at my grey suit jacket which was wet with dark patches where the heavy rain had drenched me in the short sprint from the car to the pub. But if the heavy rain continued, by the time morning came we would both be soaked through to our underwear. Bill was wearing a black suit which didn't show the wet so much. Dressing like a businessman was a necessary part of the plan, with me as driver, wearing the chauffeur's hat, while Bill would sit in the back with Lennox and keep him quiet. Bill had done a recce on Lennox's local, where he always held court every Friday with his family and cronies, and was walked home by Machete Mickey for protection, leaving the pub just after midnight. Bill thought Lennox was 'old school' since he saw him wearing a suit as he left the pub, and he reckoned the gangster always wore a suit when he went out for the evening. So with me dressed as a chauffeur, and with Bill and Lennox suited-and-booted in the back, if we were spotted or stopped by the law it might not be too much of a problem, especially as Lennox would be sedated. Just a couple of well-heeled chaps being driven home after a wizard night on the town.

I knocked back the last of my whisky and immediately fancied another, but it was going to be a long night and I needed to pace myself. I felt excited and nervous, but in spite of the bad weather forecast going according to plan, my biggest worry was being seen by someone who would call the police before I'd dealt with Lennox.

'Try not to worry,' Bill said, peering at my anxious frown. 'We've been through a lot worse.'

'Yeah,' I agreed. 'Like that caper to snatch that bank CEO's daughter in Poland after his Russian missus pissed off with her.'

Bill nodded thoughtfully as he recalled the escapade. 'And then it transpires she was in the KGB. That's what you call dicing with death. It broke my heart having to abort that mission.'

'You mean it broke your heart having to give back most of the down payment.'

Bill grinned and studied his empty whisky tumbler. 'Minus our lavish lifestyle expenses of course. Still, even though we didn't manage to snatch his daughter, the rich bastard could afford it for the risks we took.'

'Yeah, we could have ended up in some Russian gulag,' I said. 'What a risk that was. But we were a lot younger then. My biggest worry about tonight is a fisherman seeing us and calling the police on his mobile.'

Bill grinned and raised his hands to imaginary elements. 'In this weather? You must be joking.'

'Fishermen are like golfers,' I said. 'They're obsessive.'

'Well, as a golf fanatic you ought to know.'

'Exactly. Fishermen and golfers go out in all weathers.'

'Don't worry. It's pissing down so hard they'll be too busy building arks. And for once they've got the forecast right, which is why it has to be tonight. And I've done a thorough recce on the area. I doubt very much there'll be anyone around, fishermen or otherwise, at four in the morning.'

'Cheers, mate, I appreciate it.' I raised my empty glass to Bill, then banged it with reluctance onto the table, knowing there'd be no more alcohol for a while.

'And thank you for lending me the Jag to do the recces.'

I laughed. 'You could hardly do what you did using public transport, you berk. No, Bill, I mean it, I really do appreciate what you're doing for me. This is one I owe you. Big time.'

He leant sideways and patted my knee. 'You owe me nothing, Freddie. I know how much this means to you.' He glanced at his watch. 'I think we'd better make a move, just in case Lennox leaves his boozer a bit earlier.'

★

Lennox's local was somewhere between West Ham and Canning Town in a residential street. The pub was on a corner of a crossroads and Bill instructed me to park in one of the streets where he knew Lennox would be walking home, so that I was on the road side and Bill was in the passenger seat near the kerb ready to slip out once Mickey and Lennox were about to pass. I knew our biggest problem was if loads of other customers left the pub at the same time as Lennox, but Bill assured me that of the two visits he'd made, Lennox was one of the last to leave, and even if there were a couple of other stragglers, there'd be enough voltage from his torch to flatten a few drunks. No problem.

We were using a weapon we'd used loads of times in our dim and distant past. It was a flashlight stun gun, a Zaplight with a punishing 1,000,000 volts, capable of penetrating clothing. It looked like an ordinary torch, but shine it in a victim's face and, believe me, they are in for something of a shock! Instant knockout!

Bill fumbled in his pocket, took out the torch and laid it on the seat next to him. Then he took out the quarter bottle of Scotch, reached over and put it on the back seat ready for Lennox.

'What have you put in the hooch?' I asked.

'Date rape drug. GHB.'

'As long as he's compos mentis enough by 4:00 a.m. to tell me what I want to know.'

'I've only put one gram in the bottle. He won't need much of it to keep him sedated. He'll be well tanked up on a Friday night as it is. Last Friday when I come out here, he was swaying and his bodyguard was almost carrying him.'

'So we might not even need the GHB once he's had a blast from the torch.'

'Don't be stupid, Freddie. We've talked this through. He doesn't know who the fuck I am, so it doesn't matter if he sees me. But we need to keep him sedated so that he's totally disorientated, then he won't suspect this is anything to do with you. Otherwise you're either going to have to kill him, or risk his retribution on you and your family.'

I was silent for a bit, mulling it over. 'But once we question him about my dad...'

I heard Bill sighing deeply, and when he spoke, his voice in the darkness of the car sounded soft and deep but menacing, like a musical instrument reverberating as it reached the lowest note.

'He won't have a clue about anything by the time we've finished with him. Nothing. His brain'll be reduced to a pile of shit.'

I knew I could rely on my partner's professionalism, if that's what you call psychological torture. When he was in the paras he worked a tour of Northern Ireland in the seventies and his speciality was interrogation. He'd often told me that to get someone to talk all it takes is deep-rooted fear, and there was rarely any need to resort to physical torture. Discover the victim's weakness, use disorientation, and sheer terror does the rest. It was what he called the Winston Smith method, based on Orwell's *Nineteen Eighty-Four* and the rats in Room 101.

I pressed the light switch on my watch and saw it was gone twelve. As the rain pelted down and the windows misted up, visibility was a problem, especially as we needed to make a quick getaway. I could see nothing through the windscreen and switched on the hot air booster to clear it.

'Sorry if it's going to be stifling for a bit. But I can see fuck all out there.'

'It'll get even hotter in a while,' Bill sniggered. 'Then it's zap, Batters, with my trusty torch. It's what might have killed Princess Diana, you know. That spooky car that came through the tunnel in the opposite direction – all it would take would be a flash from one of these monster torches in her driver's face and – crash!'

'You don't believe all that conspiracy crap, do you?'

'Of course I don't. I'm just offering you an explanation of the means, how an assassin could do it and not get caught.'

'So it's theoretical then.'

'That's right. Stephen Hawking school of thought. Clever but not provable.'

I began to laugh, mainly from nerves, and then I felt Bill tense as he peered into the left side wing mirror and whispered, 'This is it, Freddie. They're leaving the pub.'

On this particular night Lennox must have been relatively sober because before we knew it he and his minder were almost level with the car. Bill grabbed the door handle and thrust it open. I could see Mickey Whiting had been taken by surprise, encumbered by the golf umbrella he held over his boss.

'Hey!' he shouted in surprise.

But Bill was already on his feet and shone the torch in Mickey's face. Lennox's henchman screamed as he flopped backwards in a heap, caught up in the spokes of the umbrella.

'What the fuck—' Lennox began, but was cut short by the high voltage shock of Bill's Zaplight. Bill caught him under the arms as he was about to fall, and I leant across the seat and threw open the back door. It all happened within seconds, although Bill trying to shove the stunned gangster into the back seat proved awkward, as Lennox was now a dead weight with his arms and legs thrashing about like a frenzied octopus, while his insensible moans sounded uncanny and nightmarish.

'Hurry up,' I urged. 'Before Mickey recovers.'

I turned the ignition, almost expecting it to cough, choke and die as so often happens in films at moments of crisis, but the engine purred confidently and sounded healthy. I switched the windscreen wipers onto fast, clicked on dipped headlights, put the car into drive and strained to see the road through the steamed-up windscreen and the pelting rain. From the back I heard scuffling sounds, followed by the slam of a door.

'That's it! He's in!' Bill cried. 'Go! Go! Go!'

I put my foot hard on the accelerator and we took off, my head pressed close to the windscreen as I struggled to see the road ahead and the parked cars on either side. I hoped Mickey Whiting hadn't recovered sufficiently to clock my registration number, but I think my anxiety on that score was unfounded. A zap from a high voltage flashlight like Bill had dished out would leave him wondering which planet he was on for some time yet.

When we got to the main road I turned right and headed towards the West End. I took the chauffeur's cap out of the glove compartment and stuck it on, just in case we were stopped, and dropped my speed to slightly below the limit.

A long moan from Lennox, and then he mumbled, 'Who are you, you bastards? What do you want?'

Bill chuckled. 'Don't worry, me old mate. I just want you to enjoy the ride and have a little drink with me.'

I heard him unscrewing the whisky bottle, and I adjusted my rear view mirror to see what was happening. Lennox was lying with his head back, his mouth open, trying to gulp air, his eyes blinking as he tried to bring himself round from his shocked stupor. I saw Bill stick the neck of the bottle in his mouth, and he spluttered and choked.

'Now come on,' Bill coaxed. 'You know you like a little drink on a Friday night. I got you a nice little whisky as a treat.'

'Don't like whisky. I'm a gin drinker.'

Bill laughed loudly and said, 'You ain't got much choice, sunshine.' He picked up the torch and waved it threateningly in front of Lennox's face. 'So what's it to be? Another painful zap from this stun gun or have a nice swig of this warm alcohol?'

Lennox was silent. I took my eyes from the road for a moment and watched as the gangster screwed his eyes tight like a child having medicine administered to it.

'That's better,' Bill said soothingly. 'Get it down you.'

Lennox took three large gulps of whisky, then his face contorted into a hideous gargoyle-like grimace as he complained, 'Ugh! It tastes salty.'

Bill screwed the top back on the bottle. 'OK. That's enough for now. Just lie still and enjoy the ride.'

Lennox took a trip to stupor land almost immediately and collapsed into an uncomfortable heap, squashed into a corner. I drove carefully and reached Aldgate in less than fifteen minutes. We spoke very little throughout the journey, and even when we did, we were careful not to use our names, just in case Lennox's mind registered something subliminally, although it was doubtful. His boozed, zapped and drugged brain was well and truly pulped for the next couple of hours.

From Aldgate I swung a right and went via the Angel, along past King's Cross and Euston to Westway, and it wasn't long before we reached Bill's gaff in Shepherd's Bush. By now it was almost 1:00 a.m. There were a few lights on in some of the houses in Bill's street. Apart from that the cul-de-sac was quiet and still. But as I reached the end of the street, with little space in which to turn, I hadn't been able to find a single parking space.

'I doubt anyone's going out on a filthy night like this,' Bill said. 'You mightas well double park, cos we'll be leaving in a couple of hours.'

'Shit!' I exclaimed. 'That's all very well, but I need to turn the car round for when we leave.'

Bill laughed. 'So do a six-point turn. We've got two hours to kill.'

I managed it in five, and Bill gave me a little ripple of applause.

'Nice one,' he said. 'Now let's get this wanker up to my place.'

Getting the comatose gangster out of the car was tricky, but we eventually managed it by using brute force. No sense in being gentle and considerate with a knob like Lennox. By the time we had virtually carried him to the top floor and Bill's flat, our age and lack of regular exercise showed by the way we panted and heaved from the exertion.

We shoved Lennox into the only easy chair in the flat, and his head lolled and rolled as he slept, fitful and disturbed by whatever demons haunted him, although I doubted he had a conscience. Lennox obeyed only one rule in life: don't get caught.

Bill brewed strong coffee to keep us awake and we spoke in undertones for the next two hours. Now and then Lennox stirred in his drugged sleep, his eyes half opened but he appeared not to register anything other than confusion, probably seeing everything as a blur, like someone on an acid trip. It was as Bill had predicted. He was totally disorientated.

At 3:30 Bill said, 'It'll be getting light by the time we get there. Time to hit the road.'

'You using the hood?' I asked him.

He patted his bulging pocket. 'Of course. No interrogation would complete without it. I'll put it on him when we get to our destination. Just in case we're spotted by the law.'

Which is exactly what happened. Our journey was uneventful until we reached Richmond, and then we were followed from Richmond Station, all along Paradise Road as far as Richmond Bridge by a patrol car. I saw them in my mirror talking and probably radioing enquiries to see if the Jaguar was reported as stolen. The lights were red just before Richmond Bridge, and they stopped behind us. They swerved suddenly to the left and pulled up alongside us, then looked intently into the car, peering at me through the pelting rain. I was wearing the chauffeur's hat and I turned and acknowledged them with a nod. The driver of the patrol car nodded back to me then stared at the back seat passengers. But visibility was tricky as the rain was lashing down and the side windows were damp on the inside and misted. From the corner of my eye I saw Bill, who was sitting on the left in the back, pressing his face to the window, grinning and waving at the coppers, playing the part of a pissed reveller being taken home. It must have done the trick, because the patrol car suddenly shot off straight ahead in the direction of Petersham. The filter light turned green and I turned right on to Richmond Bridge, letting my breath out slowly, feeling the tightness in my neck and shoulders loosening. It had been a tense moment and I heard Bill mutter, 'That was a close call.'

And then I heard a groan from behind me and felt a movement, a light kick and pressure on the back of my seat. Lennox was stirring.

'I think he's coming round,' Bill said. 'He'll soon be ready to answer a few questions.'

At Twickenham I turned left and headed towards Teddington, and after a mile or two Bill told me to turn left onto Broom Road and Teddington Lock. End of the road. Literally and metaphorically. The road ended at the walkway which led to the Thames. And it was time for the final confrontation after years of waiting for answers which only Lennox could provide.

We passed the pub to my right, the quaint Tide End Cottage, and parked near a building that looked like a chandler, right opposite the enormous pub garden of The Anglers. I switched the engine off and listened. All was silent outside, except for the rain drumming on the roof. But in the distance I fancied I could hear the roar of water tumbling over the weir above Teddington Lock. Although the sky was dark and heavy with rain clouds, a little dawn brightness filtered through, giving us just enough light to see our way to the river.

I turned round and looked at my passengers in the back. Lennox's head was lolling back and his tongue was protruding, tentatively licking his lips. Bill was prepared, and knew our prisoner would be dehydrated and would need a drink of water to bring him round and make him adequately alert for his impending ordeal.

Bill unscrewed the cap on a plastic bottle and put it to Lennox's lips. 'Come on, Mark. Drink this. It'll make you feel better,' he said soothingly as he tilted the water into the gangster's mouth, who spluttered and gagged. 'Take it easy.' Bill sounded as if he was a considerate friend rather than an interrogator. Lennox recovered slightly from the initial sip of water, and readily and gratefully accepted another mouthful. Once he'd had several swigs, his eyes opened, bleary and frightened.

'Who are you?' he said. 'What do you want?'

Bill nodded at me. 'He's ready. Let's do it.' He took the black hood out of his pocket and rammed it over Lennox's head. Muffled protests from the gangster as Bill bundled him out of the car. He almost fell onto the tarmac, but I was already out of the car and caught him under his other arm. He tried to walk, but sometimes we had to carry his dead weight as his feet dragged along the ground, along past the pub garden towards the steps leading to the bridge which crossed over to the lock and the south side of the river. Just before we got to the steps leading to the bridge, another few steps led down to a path, now squelching and thick with mud. We crossed under the bridge, along the path winding through the trees, and we heard it now, in full flood, the roar of the thousands of tons of water tumbling over the weir.

I felt Lennox stiffen and he tried to pull back, away from the petrifying sound of what he feared most, the vast and watery noise of death. On one side of the river, to our left as we faced upstream, the gentler waters filtering into the lock, calm and tranquil like a canal, unlike the terrifying mass of water plunging over the weir as we stood facing it on the promontory which divided the river.

I could see the water cascading over the weir, frothing and foaming, awesome in its destructive power, and I tried to imagine what Lennox must have felt in the darkness of his hood, picturing in his black imagination a catastrophic end, but aware that what was happening was all too real.

His body quivered and shook, the tremors increasing, so that I thought he might collapse and die before I had the answers I needed. Muffled by the hood, he begged and pleaded, and I could hear him sobbing like a child.

'Listen to me, Lennox,' I shouted over the roar of the water, 'I'll let you go – get you away from the water – if you tell me about Charles Weston. You blackmailed him, and he topped himself.'

'I didn't! I didn't!' he cried. 'I promise you, Freddie, I didn't do nothing to him.'

Fuck! The disorientation hadn't worked. He knew who I was.

I gripped him tighter, my nails digging into his arms, which shivered and rippled like crazy. He was like a volcano of fear about to erupt and go berserk.

'Don't lie to me, you slimy bastard. We found a note at my mother's house. You blackmailed him, you bastard. Took all his savings. Bled him dry. Now I want to know why.'

'You don't want to know. You really don't want to know.'

'That's where you're wrong, Lennox,' I shouted above the noise of the torrent. 'I've got the proof you blackmailed my father, and I want to know why.'

He shook violently. 'Get me away from here, Freddie. Please! I'll do anything. Anything you want.'

'Listen to all that water, Lennox. And you are going for a fucking swim. So tell me.'

'Please, Freddie!'

I grabbed him by the lapels and shoved him closer to the edge of the embankment. 'This is it, Lennox. Last fucking chance.'

'No, Freddie!' he screamed. 'Get me away from here and I'll tell you.'

I spun him around away from the edge. 'So tell me, you fucker. Why did you blackmail my old man?'

'It was someone in the Kray firm. They had photos of him and them.'

This made no sense. What was my old man's connection with Ronnie and Reggie Kray, the notorious sixties gangsters?

I squeezed the lapels tighter on Lennox's suit. 'What the fuck you on about? What photos?'

'Someone in the Kray firm took 'em. Photos of Ronnie, this politician and your old man. A threesome.'

A jagged slash, an icicle of revulsion. I felt myself submerged and drowning in raging waters of disgust. 'You're fucking lying, Lennox,' I screamed.

'I'm not. Your old man was a shirt-lifter. Caught on camera being buggered by Ronnie while he sucked this politician's cock.' Fear, trauma and stress brought out Lennox's truly repulsive and offensive character as he became sickeningly aggressive and outspoken. 'Your old man was nothing more than a brown-hatter, a fucking bum bandit who liked nothing better than being fucked up the arse by cunts like Ronnie Kray.'

Although he couldn't see me, Lennox could sense I was about to freak, and pulled away from me. The momentum took him backwards towards steps leading down to the channel flowing into the lock. I was about to go after him, to pummel and smash him, but one fraction of a second he was poised at the top of the steps, and the next moment he had disappeared.

I heard a muffled scream followed by a splash, and stood rooted to the spot, numb from the awful truth.

I had forgotten Bill in all this, who suddenly grabbed my elbow and shook my arm urgently. 'He'll drown, Freddie. You can't let it happen.'

'Serve the bastard right,' I yelled.

'Life imprisonment for murder! Is that what you want?'

'You get him. I'm fucked if I will.'

I stood in a daze, stuck to the squelching mud of the bank, and watched Bill take off. He disappeared down the steps to the channel, and I heard choking cries and agitated splashing sounds as Lennox struggled to survive. After a moment I saw Bill's hunched figure as he struggled backwards, pulling Lennox by the arms to the safety of the muddy bank. He laid Lennox on his back then turned to stare at me.

'I'm sorry, Freddie,' he said. 'What you might call an eventful night.' And then he laughed, whether it was out of nervousness and embarrassment or an attempt to defuse the situation, I have no idea. 'Come on, Freddie. Get it together, mate. We've been in worse situations than this. Remember Angola?'

I nodded dumbly, still trying to recover from the shock. Bill took charge, and I was grateful he did because I was still suffering from Lennox's terrible thunderbolt.

'We can't leave this bastard here – much as I know you'd like to. Give me a hand to get him back to the car.'

I moved like an automaton towards him. 'I'll be OK, Bill. I'm just...' I could feel tears welling up.

Bill noticed and patted my arm. 'I know how it is, mate. But it's over now.'

We hauled Lennox to his feet and struggled back to the car. He must have been in a state of shock, because not a sound came from him. He was semi-conscious, although tremors moved like waves lapping through his body at intervals.

I drove back in silence, and I was grateful to Bill for not speaking. I drove over Kew Bridge and along Chiswick High Road, and we were almost at Hammersmith when Bill first spoke.

'Jesus! I'm soaked through, and it's not just cos of the rain. I've been for an early swim.'

'I'm pretty wet myself,' I said. 'What shall we do with our passenger?'

'Drop him off in a side street between Hammersmith and Shepherd's Bush Green, then we can go back to my place. I can get changed and you can get cleaned up.'

We turned into a street of terrace houses. It wasn't yet 5:00 a.m. and no one in the street appeared to be stirring; even milkmen seemed to be a thing of the past now, so we bundled Lennox out onto the pavement and left him there.

When we got back to Bill's, he stuck the kettle on to make us coffee, then changed out of his wet lounge suit while I washed the mud off my shoes in the sink.

As soon as we were sat sipping hot coffee, Bill said, 'You have to get things into perspective, Freddie.'

I remembered Michelle telling me that about Jackie and I could almost guess what he would say.

'If it happened in this day and age, what your old man was up to back then, it would be tolerated, Freddie. No question about it. But I guess when that photo was taken, it was still a criminal act. They didn't decriminalise homosexuality until towards the end of the sixties.'

'I know, but I hate to think of my old man with Ronnie Kray.' I shivered and pulled a face. 'Monster like that. If my old man discovered he was gay and had an affair with a decent man I could come to terms with it. But he was Ronnie Kray's rough trade. Jesus Christ! That's appalling.'

'I know it is, mate. But what your old man did... I mean... I don't know how to say this but as it was still illegal then, and gays had no way of openly meeting other gays, I guess people made terrible mistakes. Formed relationships they later regretted.'

I could feel anger building up inside me again. 'But now I know why he topped himself, I think I hate my father even more.'

'You never told me you hated him before?'

'Maybe I was in denial. But I think deep down I hated him for not facing up to what he was frightened of, instead of killing himself.' I sighed deeply. 'What a fucking mess.'

Bill gave me a sympathetic smile. 'Well, it's over now, Freddie. You've got a family you love, and I know you always put them first, so now maybe it's time to bury the past, mate.'

'Time to bury Lennox, the fucking bastard. I hope the bastard dies of pneumonia.'

'But when he recovers, Freddie, you could be in big trouble.'

Frowning deeply, Bill got up, went to his laptop desk, pulled open the bottom drawer, rummaged under a bundle of papers and took out a small pistol and a box of cartridges.

'A Glock 26,' I said as he walked towards me, offering me the gun.

'Small but effective. You'd better take it and the box of ammo. I'm sorry, mate, I was wrong about the disorientation, and pretty soon Lennox is going to send someone to get you. You're going to need this for protection.'

I waved it aside and shook my head. 'Half-term has just started. I'll go home and take the family away for a surprise holiday.'

'And then what?'

'I'll cross that bridge when I come to it.'

'Freddie, don't be an idiot. Lennox isn't going to forget what we put him through tonight. He's going to want his revenge.'

'I shook my head even more emphatically. 'I'll do everything in my power to protect my family. But I'm a civilian now, and I'm not going to start waving guns around.'

'Even to protect your family?'

I thought about it for a while. I could escape for a week and no one in Lennox's outfit would know where the hell I'd gone. But once I got home the threat would be there, hanging over me and my family. And my family was everything to me.

So I took the gun.

★

Having stopped at a café to have the full English breakfast, I drove the Jag to a small lot at the back of a Homebase store north of Islington, where Polish migrants offered a good valet and car wash at a reasonable price. Even though it was still raining, I still needed the car cleaned as it was in a filthy state. The bodywork was spattered with all kinds of shit, and the inside was even worse with great dollops of mud from the river bank all over the carpets and on the back seat where Lennox had lain. But after the conscientious Poles had finished with it, it was acceptable as a vehicle that had been driven only in London rain and been nowhere near a river in full flood.

I waited until nine-thirty then rang Michelle, who was worried and wondered why I hadn't climbed between the sheets in the early hours. I told her the car had broken down, the AA had got me started, but I needed to get to a garage and get a new starter motor put in for our trip to Brittany for the half term holiday. It came as a great surprise to her as we'd had nothing planned, and when I explained that it could be one of the last holidays we might have together as a family, seeing as Jackie would soon be eighteen, Michelle got very excited and said she would probably be out by the time I got back, shopping and making preparations for the trip. I told her we would leave at teatime, drive through the tunnel, and maybe spend the night in Le Touquet, have a meal and frequent the casino, then on Sunday continue to Dinan, one of our favourite towns in France.

I thought this trip would give me breathing space, and I guessed that by the time someone found the semi-conscious gangster in Hammersmith, had him admitted to hospital and then identified – and it would probably take him a while to recover – I'd have a good twenty-four hours at least until he might start planning his revenge, by which time we'd be in France.

But who was I kidding? It would be temporary respite, that was all. I still had to face my unpredictable future, which was hanging by a very thin piece of thread.

16

BORN AGAIN

My eyes snapped open and I was suddenly wide awake. Beside me, Michelle sat bolt upright, then shook me by the shoulder.

'Freddie!' she whispered. 'I heard something.'

I sat up and listened intently but could hear no sound, either from outside the house or inside. 'Are you sure you heard something?'

'Yeah, I'm sure. It sounded like someone trying to get in the back door.'

Our first night back from France and the nightmare had begun. The moment I'd been fearing all week. A week where I'd been unable to concoct a single plan to counter Lennox's offensive, other than to save my family by sacrificing myself. And the only way Lennox would satisfy his lust for blood was by handing out the ultimate retribution. My termination. But first he would want to pull me apart, bit by painful bit. He would want me to suffer before I croaked and, with an evil bastard like Lennox, I knew it would be long and lingering.

'There it is again!' Michelle hissed. 'You must have heard it, Freddie.'

A scraping sound and I could have sworn it was coming from the back door. 'Sounds like a burglar,' I whispered. 'I'd better take a look.'

I felt Michelle's fingernails digging into my arm. 'Freddie! Be careful!'

'Stay there. Don't worry, I'll creep down and arm myself with a broom handle.'

It was a dark, moonless night, but I didn't dare switch the light on. I sleep naked and there was no way I was going to confront one of Lennox's henchmen in the nude, so I struggled to slip on a pair of jeans and a sweatshirt.

'What are you doing?' Michelle murmured.

'Putting some clothes on.'

'For God's sake, Freddie! Just go downstairs, switch the light on and make a lot of noise. Shout out that you're calling the police.'

'I feel fucking vulnerable in the nude,' I hissed, fear gripping me now like a vice as I struggled into a pair of denims, tucking my wedding tackle clear as I zipped the fly. I hastily shoved a sweatshirt over my head and whispered, 'That's it! I'm on my way.'

'Freddie! Be careful!'

I tiptoed downstairs and crept into the living room, felt my way to a corner of the room near some electric sockets and moved an occasional table away from the corner. I pulled back the carpet, raised the loose floorboard, and about a foot along, where the electric cables ran, felt for the gun I'd hidden there. I made certain the safety catch was off before hurrying through to the kitchen. I padded through the utility room, almost wishing the door had been glass. It was pitch black and I could hear a systematic scraping noise.

I felt my way to the door, my hand gripping the gun tightly, my finger poised over the trigger. I realised I had a major problem if I was going to surprise whoever was on the patio. There was a key in the lock and a bolt high up, which meant I had to slide the bolt with my left hand, then turn the key in the lock before I could open the door. But whoever was on the other side would be alerted before I could complete the action.

Although the scratching had stopped, I could hear a faint noise, a padding sound, as if someone was treading stealthily on the patio, perhaps searching for a weakness at one of the kitchen windows or the French windows round the corner. I placed my ear close against the door and strained for any clue as to where the person might be now, but I couldn't be certain if what I was hearing was someone breathing or moving about.

Hopefully the person on the other side, if he was armed, wouldn't be expecting me to be kneeling on the floor and would aim high. So, having placed the gun on the floor, I stretched and reached the bolt, took a deep breath as I felt for the key, slammed the bolt across with my left hand, twisted the key, and dropped to a squatting position as I picked up the gun and pulled the door open.

A shadow darted across the patio, down the steps and across the lawn as I took aim. It was gone in an instant, and thankfully I didn't have to wake the entire neighbourhood with a gunshot. I clicked the safety catch on, locked the kitchen door, concealed the gun under the floorboard and tiptoed back to our bedroom.

'What was it?' Michelle whispered, he voice quivering with fright, as I got undressed.

'It was an opportunist burglar,' I said.

'What?'

'Yeah, one with a bushy tail.'

'Oh, is that all? Those foxes are getting so bloody cheeky now.'

I climbed back into bed, kissed Michelle goodnight and lay back, eyes wide open, seeing nothing but dark shadows weaving about. Although I was relieved it had been a false alarm, I was still worried sick and I agonised about my complicated situation for the rest of the night, even though my brain longed for sleep.

★

A week passed in which nothing happened, a week in which I hardly ventured out. Whenever I did, it was a nightmare of fear and paranoia, wondering when Lennox would send one of his thugs to get me. I thought it odd he hadn't attempted anything so far and wondered if the disorientation had worked and he had forgotten who it was who had snatched him.

I relied mainly on Jack to conduct the practical day-to-day running of the business and told Michelle I was starting to slow down. She seemed pleased, knowing I was going to be at home most nights, and I tried to hide my nervousness by talking and joking, overdoing the banter and stories as if I was high on something. But I don't think Michelle, Jackie or Olivia noticed anything unusual in my behaviour, even though I noticed myself over-compensating for my edginess and I became more and more hyper as each day passed.

The gun remained hidden under the floorboards and hadn't been brought out once since the fox incident, but it was there for when and if I needed it.

As I nervously entered the second week as a housebound husband, I knew I was going to have to get on with life, otherwise my business might suffer. Michelle knew I was getting restless, and I think she wanted me to get back to some semblance of normality and she'd probably had enough of my almost manic behaviour.

I decided it was high time I did the rounds of my West End clubs, and I'd heard from Jack that Phil the Greek at the Jax wanted to see me to discuss using my organisation to provide doormen for his club. It was perfect timing because Michelle had arranged to take her mother to a caravan park in Felixstowe for the weekend and Olivia agreed go with them. Jackie had a new boyfriend who lived in Chiswick with his parents and she was going there for Friday and Saturday and would be returning on the Sunday.

On Friday night, with the family safely away, I got the gun from its hiding place, stuck it in a padded brown envelope, and put it in the glove compartment of my car. It was just after 8:00 p.m. when I reached the West End, and I found a parking space in Golden Square. The weather was still piss-poor, with heavy and frequent showers. I was caught by one just as I turned into Regent Street, and darted into a shop doorway to shelter for a few minutes. And that was when I spotted Machete Mickey diving into a shop doorway further up the street.

It was no coincidence, and I cursed myself for having lost concentration on the drive from my house to the West End. The only way Mickey could have followed me was from home. The chances of finding me here in the centre of London would have been impossible. He must have driven behind me all the way and I'd been too careless to notice.

My gun was in the car, but there was no way I could use it in the middle of Regent Street on a Friday night. And then I saw his massive figure coming out of his hiding place and lumbering along the wide pavement towards me. I was frozen with fear, wondering if he had his machete concealed beneath the long raincoat he wore. All it would take would be a few slashes, my hands would be cut to ribbons trying to protect my face, then one quick slash and my throat would be cut.

He was only yards away, and I prepared to run. If I could make it to the Liquid Velvet, less than five-hundred yards from where I was standing, I might be safe. And I could rely on Jack, who was a martial arts expert, to come to my assistance.

I got ready to run as I'd never run before. But then I heard Mickey call out, 'Hold up, Freddie! I'd like a word.'

There was something about his reasonable tone that halted me. Or was I being stupid again? Perhaps Mickey was brighter than I'd ever given him credit for, and maybe his tone was a trick to keep me from running off.

But as he got close to me I noticed his hands hung loose at his sides, and his coat was unbuttoned and flapped open, revealing nothing underneath other than his ample belly.

'Sorry I had to follow you, Freddie, but I need to speak to you. Let me buy you a drink.'

I was gobsmacked. Lennox's toughest henchman offering to buy me a drink. It didn't add up. And in the bright, Regent Street lights, I saw in his expression a faithful-dog look, wounded and seeking redemption. I was suddenly very curious indeed and I took him up on his offer.

★

We found a corner of a Mayfair pub which wasn't too crowded, sat opposite each other, and Mickey raised his pint to me tentatively, as if he was in some way apologising for past misdemeanours, although he and I had never crossed swords.

'So what's on your mind, Mickey?' I said.

'I knew you was always enemies with Mark but that's all over now.'

I was intrigued and waited for him to elaborate.

'He ain't gonna harm no one no more.'

'Oh? Why's that, Mickey?'

'He's gone barmy. Been admitted into a home. Had some sort of stroke they said. They found him soaking wet, cos of all that rain, in Hammersmith of all places. And no one had a clue how he got there.

Except me. Some little geezer snatched him earlier in the night. Knocked me out wiv a stun gun he did.'

Mickey took a sip of his pint and stared at me knowingly. 'But don't worry, Freddie, I ain't told no one else in the firm. I said I saw him home as usual and that was that.'

'I don't understand, Mickey. Why would you do that?'

''Cos I told Mark months ago that what he asked me to do was out of order. It was sinful. I'd started to have nightmares about some of the things I done to people on Mark's behalf. I used to wake up after shouting in my sleep. I could see the fear and pain in their faces. It haunted me. And then I told my cousin Sheila about it. Sheila was – well, she was one of the God squad – an' she takes me along to meet their minister – he ain't like a typical vicar – dresses normally. But he's a pukka bloke. And what he told me made so much sense. That everyone can be saved. It ain't too late for no one. I've done terrible things in my time but now I can have another chance and make things right with God. Already I feel much better, Freddie, you wouldn't believe it.'

Well, well, well. So Machete Mickey had been saved. I suppressed a smile and asked him how others in the firm had reacted to him seeing the light and absconding along the path of righteousness, although I didn't quite put it that way.

'They told me to fuck off and good riddance. I think since Mark has lost his memory things have started to fall apart. I went to see Mark in the home, cos Phil – that's the minister – said forgiveness is not an option but a necessity if you want to discover the truth. But there wasn't much point in going. I don't think Mark knew who I was. His memory's completely fucked. He thought I was his old man from way back. So that's that.'

I grinned at Mickey. 'A new beginning, eh?'

His eyes lit up as he spoke. 'Yeah, something like that. And for the first time in my life I've got a proper grafting job, working in a breaker's yard.'

'I appreciate you telling me all this, Mickey. But d'you mind if I ask you why?'

'Well, I knew you'd be worried after what happened to Mark, thinking he'd come after you.'

'Why would he do that? I mean, why me? He had loads of enemies.'

'Please, Freddie, don't treat me like an idiot. I'm not stupid, yuh know.'

'No, I'm sorry, Mickey. I guess I underestimated you.'

And it was true. I'd always thought of him as being a bit of a simpleton, but I now realised he was just a gullible bloke who could be easily manipulated. I suppose he looked on Lennox's firm as an evil family who looked after their own and he knew no better. And now the firm's head of the family was gone, he had to find another family, only this time he had found it in the church and redemption at last. It might be another form of manipulation but at least he wouldn't carve people up any more, much as they might deserve it.

But the brightest aspect of this whole affair was the fact that I was off the hook. I could have hugged Mickey for this piece of news. My troubles were over. I could move on at last.

★

The conclusion to this episode was my visit to Mum. Like me, I knew the only way she could move on was by knowing why Dad was being blackmailed by Lennox. So I sat opposite her at her kitchen table and began the long and involved tale of my snatching Lennox just over a week ago. She listened intently, not saying a word. Her eyes were watery and bloodshot, and a pint glass of water stood on the table in front of her, clearly a remedy for dehydration after imbibing too many gins.

When I got to the reason for Lennox's blackmail, I couldn't bring myself to tell her about the threesome with Ronnie Kray and the politician, so instead I told her a half-truth: that Lennox had discovered Dad was gay and had a photograph to prove it.

After I hit her with this – what I thought was a bombshell – she didn't speak while she digested the information. Finally, after a long and uncomfortable pause, her frowning expression was one of sheer disbelief.

'You mean your father killed himself just because he was gay?'

I nodded and she laughed uncertainly.

'Why would anyone commit suicide because they're going to be exposed as gay? It don't make sense. You only have to look at people on television – that Graham Norton, and then there's George Michael and…'

I interrupted her before she ran the full gamut of gays in the media. 'Different era, Mum. In the sixties, up until 1967, homosexuality was against the law.'

'Yes, but even so.' She shrugged, still finding it hard to comprehend why anyone would want to commit suicide over it.

'And Lennox,' I explained, 'would have really put the frighteners on Dad. Who knows what terrible things he said to him, making him feel ashamed and desperate.'

'That Lennox was an evil bastard, Freddie.'

'Well, if it's any consolation, Mum, he's finally got what he deserves.'

She smacked the table with the flat of her hand. 'If you ask me, he's got off scot-free.'

'How d'you work that out?'

'Because there's lots of very good people in homes all over the country who have got Alzheimer's. So Lennox is just the same as anyone else who's got the disease. He won't be able to remember any of his evil acts. He'll be just like the rest of them.'

'Even if he did remember,' I said, 'I doubt he'd give it a second thought. Except to gloat, maybe. Blokes like Lennox don't have a conscience.'

'True.' She patted my hand. 'Would you like a cup of tea, son?'

'Tea?' I said, my jaw almost hitting the table.

'Yeah, a nice cuppa. I probably drink too much gin. Might as well take it easy.'

She didn't see the huge grin on my face as she went into the kitchen to fill the kettle. It was a positive beginning and, although there are countless people who might criticise me for the way I handled this whole affair, taking the law into my own hands and interrogating Lennox the way I did, it wasn't something I would regret.

'D'you take sugar?' Mum asked as she lit the kettle. 'I seem to have forgotten.'

I laughed loudly as I said, 'Mum! This must be the first time in years you've offered me tea. No sugar, thanks!'

★

Apart from the usual squabbles and disagreements self-employed people experience, the next three months became uneventful and routine. Since my clashes with gangsters like Crystal and Lennox, I think I might have become a bit of an adrenaline junkie, so I was now finding the day-to-day running of my business tedious.

And then, in late October, two things happened that would change my life. Firstly, the *Sunday Express* came to an out-of-court settlement and Sid sent my fifty per cent share, which came to just over 40K. And then a client of mine, a club in South Kensington, suspected staff of big-time fiddling but couldn't discover how it was happening. They asked me for help and I employed Bill Turner there as a doorman and, as an insider, he was able to solve the problem and the chiselling staff were dismissed.

The club owners were pleased with the speedy result, paid me well for my services, which was when I had the idea of setting up my own private enquiry agency, with Bill as a working partner. The business of supplying doormen to clubs pretty much runs itself and with all the contacts I had on the club scene I thought I could secure a great deal of investigative work. When I suggested my plan to Bill, following his success in exposing the fiddling club employees, he thought it was a great idea and I began to make plans to set up the new business, which we eventually decided to call Weston and Turner Investigations. Not very imaginative but we were worried we might inadvertently use another organisation's name.

Then, we spent hours in the pub, scheming and hurling ideas at one another and often we'd end up in fits of laughter as we referred to ourselves incongruously as gumshoes, private eyes, sleuths and shamuses.

But, joking apart, I could picture the scene.

Lightning Source UK Ltd.
Milton Keynes UK
UKOW04f1140130913

217085UK00004B/11/P